*How easy it is to let conviction become pride.
But how rewarding it is when we hear the
whisper of Thy sweet, still voice in the midnight
and finally stretch out a hand and find it
grasped by the fingers of a friend.*

Prudence Willard
Marietta, Ohio
May 20, 1861

SECRETS OF WAYFARERS INN

All the Inn's a Stage

ROSEANNA M. WHITE

Guideposts

New York

Secrets of Wayfarers Inn is a trademark of Guideposts.

Published by Guideposts Books & Inspirational Media
110 William Street
New York, NY 10038
Guideposts.org

Cover and interior design by Müllerhaus
Cover illustration by Greg Copeland, represented by Deborah Wolfe, LTD.
Typeset by Aptara, Inc.

Printed and bound in the United States of America
10 9 8 7 6 5 4 3

Chapter One

Marietta, Ohio
May 20, 1861

Prudence Willard sidestepped another pedestrian hurrying by and clutched her shopping basket tighter. There was much to do on this Monday morning, to be sure, and it seemed many of her neighbors had not yet learned the old adage that haste made waste. What was everyone's hurry today?

"It's the *Gilded Palace!*"

The excited shout, delivered almost directly in her ear as an adolescent boy jostled by her, seemed to be aimed at someone across the street, but it might as well have been a hammerblow directly to her heart. Her feet stopped, her throat tightened, and she couldn't convince her breath to fill her chest.

They were back. Ten years later, they were back. Prudence's mind swam. They'd thought the worst, she and Jason. Feared it. Accepted it. Mourned it.

But they were back.

A boy across the street ran over to his friend, now a few steps ahead of her. "Are they doing a show? I hope it's not Shakespeare. Though Ma will only let me go if it *is*."

"Bet they'll be announcing it. Might even have papers for us to hand out—Jimmy said he got to do that last time. They paid him two whole pennies for it."

The prospect of a paying job was apparently enough enticement to spur the youths onward at a reckless pace.

Prudence sucked in a breath and forced her own feet onward, more sedately. She had errands to finish. Then the mending and ironing to do. She hadn't time to scurry down to the docks with the rest of Marietta to discover if the *Gilded Palace* had come to do another show. And even if she did, there was no guarantee that Virgil was still with the company—or that the same company still owned the boat.

But the mere thought of him being in town made her decide that she didn't really need that new spool of thread today, after all. Next week would be soon enough. After a wagon lumbered by, she crossed the street, her feet aimed for home. She had to be the one to tell Jason, before someone else could mention it in his hearing.

"Prudence? Is that you, all grown up?"

The voice halted her just as she was cutting down an alleyway. It had been a decade since she'd heard it, it was true. But one didn't forget the voice of the person responsible for the maiming of the man one loved. Ever so slowly, she turned to face him. "Virgil Sullivan. Thee has finally returned."

Janice Eastman hummed the final notes of "'Tis So Sweet to Trust in Jesus" as she snipped the thread, freeing the shimmering fabric from her sewing machine. She held up the costume, shook it out, and smiled. Turned out pretty well, if she did say so herself.

"Hey, Janice. Have a minute?"

Janice stood, holding up the silver flapper-style dress as Tess walked into Janice's sitting/sewing room. "What do you think?"

Tess Wallace drew near with a smile significantly dimmer than usual. She nodded, even reached out to run appreciative fingers down the side of the dress, but her smile didn't brighten. "Beautiful, as expected. But..."

Janice lifted her brows. "But what?"

Tess sighed. "But all this effort might be wasted. I'm not sure the show will go on."

Janice laughed because her business partner and longtime friend *must* be joking. "Right. In all the years I've known Heidi Ingram, she has not *once* canceled a performance." On the contrary, when the theater teacher put on a show at the high school, everyone in town knew they could count on it being fantastic. It was why Janice, Tess, and the third member of their triad, LuAnn Sherrill, hadn't had any qualms about hosting the debut of Heidi's new enterprise. The Wayfarers Inn would make the perfect backdrop for her traveling murder mystery dinner theater. Plus, it would mean a weekend of guaranteed revenue for the inn.

Tess crossed her arms over her middle and surveyed the growing rack of costumes that Janice had designed and sewn.

for the event. It had been fun, being the costume department again. She'd done it countless times for the high school theater department before she retired, and frankly, she'd missed it.

Tess shook her head. "I'm sure if this were another high school or community production that didn't have to actually earn money, it would go off without a hitch. But this is a business, and I've been monitoring the ticket sales."

Janice grinned and slid the silver dress onto a hanger. Tess, the business mind of their inn, had been doing more than *monitoring* the ticket sales. She had set up an online system for purchasing them and had been taking any phone orders too, here at the inn. "I'm aware."

Tess stepped closer and lowered her voice, though they were the only two up here—aside from Tom and Huck, the cat and small dog currently curled up together in a patch of sunlight, snoozing. "She said she had to sell twenty tickets to break even, right? Preferably thirty. But she's only sold six. *Six!* And that was to her out-of-town family!"

The family that would be staying here for the weekend of the production. Janice let out a slow breath and did some quick calculations. Today was Tuesday, the seventh of May. The show was scheduled for the eighteenth. "She still has almost two weeks until the play."

"I know, but..." Tess stood back and shook her head, her eyes gleaming with that sad light that said *I know the numbers, and this is bad.* "I thought maybe you could talk to her. Make sure she knows that this needs to be addressed. Tickets have been on sale for a month, and for no orders to come in other than her own family is pretty depressing. I hate to see her and her team—and you—putting so much effort into the launch of a business that's just going to flop before it even gets started."

Janice put the hanger on the rack with a click of metal on metal. She didn't have to ask why Tess thought Janice should be the one to talk to Heidi. Heidi was Janice's friend, after all—they'd taught in the same school for years, and she'd been the one to suggest to Heidi that the inn could be a great venue for her new traveling theater's debut run. It had to be a hit, to show other businesses in town how profitable it could be for them to hire the theater company for their own special events.

She turned back to Tess with pursed lips. "All right. I'll talk to her when she comes by this afternoon to work on setup."

Tess's smile looked even tighter than it had when she'd come in. "She's here now, down in the library. That's why I came to find you."

With only one longing look at the shimmering blue fabric waiting on her worktable, ready to be turned into another 1920s-era costume, Janice drew in a bolstering breath and headed for the door. "This ought to be fun."

"Now." Tess patted her shoulder. "Just put on your pastor's wife face. Kind and encouraging but no-nonsense."

Janice had certainly perfected said face over the years, before Lawrence died and made that part of her life obsolete. Thank the Lord that He gave her and Tess and LuAnn the idea for turning this old building back into an inn, or she didn't know how she'd be occupying her days now.

She and Tess walked together to the stairs and started down from their fourth-floor living quarters, all the way to the ground floor of Wayfarers Inn. Had they turned right at the bottom of the sweeping central staircase, they would have entered the soup café—closed after the lunch crowd had left—and then the kitchen. But instead they turned to the left, toward the parlor and library area, where the baby grand piano gleamed in the afternoon light, begging her to come and tickle its ivories.

Maybe she'd find some time later, before she went back to her sewing.

Assuming there was a point to going back to her sewing. She pasted on a smile that she hoped looked a little brighter than Tess's and strode into the room, toward the shelves where she spotted Heidi's golden-blond hair pulled back in a rare ponytail.

Janice stopped short when she saw the black T-shirt and jeans her friend wore. Usually, Heidi decked herself out in the closest thing to high fashion a fifty-year-old high school teacher could reasonably get away with. "Hi, Heidi."

At the greeting, Heidi spun, cables in her hands and a wide smile on her face. The day's makeup still adorned her face, complete with long lashes that Janice always suspected were fake…not that she'd ever dared to ask.

"Janice, hey! You're just in time. I could use an extra set of hands, and Leila's still a few minutes away."

Janice couldn't keep from bristling at the name. When she'd realized that Leila Johnson was on Heidi's cast, she'd taken her friend aside and asked if that was a good idea, knowing Heidi would remember that Leila had been the suspected culprit behind a particularly mean-spirited prank in Janice's classroom during her last year of teaching. Heidi had assured her Leila was all sweetness and talent. And no one had ever *proven* she'd been the one to sabotage each and every one of Janice's sewing machines.

She ought to give the girl the benefit of the doubt. She *would*. And so she covered the bristling with a smile. "What do you need me to do?"

"Could you hold these cables in place here while I run the other ends up along the top of the bookshelves?" Heidi motioned with her head toward the stepladder set up a few feet away.

"Sure." Janice cast a look at Tess—or tried to, but Tess was scurrying away. Maybe she'd heard the phone ring. Tucking a curl behind her ear, Janice crouched down to anchor the black cables on the floor.

Heidi was really going all out, rigging special effects all over the inn for the performance. It would be quite a show…if anyone showed up to see it. Janice drew in a breath, gave herself a pep talk, and decided to get it over with. "You're sure Leila can be trusted?"

Or maybe put it off for just a minute more.

"Hmm? Oh." Heidi hooked the stepladder with a foot, dragged it closer, and climbed up. "Look, I know she was the most likely suspect for that sewing machine thing, given that she dropped your class the day before. But seriously, Janice, she's a sweetheart. I don't think she did it. And even if she did, that was three years ago. Kids change a lot between freshman and senior years."

"Yeah, I know." Janice had certainly seen that plenty of times in her years of teaching. She held the cables still against a tug and made it a point not to peer around the bookcase at her friend. "As long as you're sure."

"I'm sure. She's a great kid. Very talented."

At texting, anyway. The other night when she had come over with the rest of Heidi's cast, she hadn't once put her phone down. Janice sighed and scolded herself for the mean-spirited thought. "I'm sure she is."

The bell at the front door jangled, which wouldn't have made her come to attention, except that LuAnn called out, "Get a load of this, guys!"

Janice didn't release the cables, but she did angle her body so she could see as LuAnn and Tess came into the room along with Brad Grimes carrying a large cardboard box in his arms.

Janice raised her eyebrows. "She putting you to work again, Brad?"

Their friend and Realtor grinned—and aimed it mostly at LuAnn, as usual. "I was chatting with LuAnn outside when Harry Olson dropped this off."

LuAnn looked absolutely giddy over whatever it was, going so far as to clap her hands. "Set it down anywhere, Brad, so we can open it."

Janice lifted her gaze toward Tess, who rolled her eyes and said, "Books."

Janice smiled. "Ah. That explains the craziness."

LuAnn was their resident literature and history buff, having just retired last year from her career as an English teacher.

The box certainly looked historical, which was a kind way of saying it was ready to fall apart. Janice asked the obvious question. "Why did Harry drop off a box of books?"

LuAnn didn't peel her eyes off the box as Brad lowered it gingerly to the floor. "He said some people were clearing out their attic and came across it, brought it to the antique mall. He has a hard time moving books but took them when he saw that they were all from Riverfront House."

Well, that did make them more interesting. They'd found plenty of things that had belonged to the original hotel in this building, but never books.

Tess leaned closer to peek inside. "How did he know they came from here?"

Brad opened the box, and LuAnn pulled out a book. She flipped through the first few pages. "My guess would be this 'Property of Riverfront House Hotel' stamp on the title page."

Heidi chuckled and continued tucking cables along the top of the shelf. "That's a good indicator. And hey, LuAnn, I wanted to thank you for your edits on my script. They were great!"

That actually pulled LuAnn's gaze off the book in her hand. "Oh, I'm glad you thought so. I was a little leery of suggesting such big changes to your plot, but..."

"No, I'm glad you did. It makes it so much more compelling. I already emailed the update to the cast. Dempsey won't be too happy that her part has shrunk, but I'll promise her a bigger role in next month's production."

Janice exchanged a glance with Tess, who lifted her brows. Her question was clear. *Did you talk to her yet?*

Janice gave her a sheepish shrug and rolled her eyes toward LuAnn and Brad and the interruption.

Heidi climbed down from the stepladder, moved it a few feet farther away, and climbed back up. "Almost done, Janice."

"No rush." She watched as LuAnn pulled out book after book, arranging them in piles that Janice couldn't detect the rhyme or reason to from this distance. Perhaps fiction and non-fiction. Or subject. Or condition. No doubt the nice ones would find a place on these very shelves beside which Janice was crouching, but some looked as battered as the box. "Anything good in there, Lu?"

"I haven't heard of most of them, but there are a few I recognize. A volume of Shakespeare, some poetry, that sort of thing." LuAnn pulled out an oversized but thin book and set it on the floor separate from the others. "I doubt that one would even fit on a shelf. Not upright, anyway."

Tess picked it up. "Mother Goose rhymes! How fun. I bet there are some good illustrations in here." She opened it up and then frowned. "Um..." She pulled out the pages. Just lifted them right out, as if they hadn't been bound in there at all.

Maybe they hadn't—the slender stack of yellowed paper wasn't quite the same size as the book and seemed to have a separate back cover of faded blue.

"What in the world?" LuAnn reached for the pages that Tess held out to her. "Odd. Definitely not Mother Goose. It looks like a script for a play. Part of one, anyway."

"A *what?*" As if LuAnn had spoken the magic word, Heidi jumped down from the ladder and flew to her side, all but dancing. "Can I see it? Can I? Please?"

LuAnn handed it over with a laugh. "Have at it."

"No front cover. I wonder what play it's for." Heidi flipped through a few pages, her eyes skimming over the lines. "I don't recognize it. Definitely just a fragment though. Looks like we don't have anything before page twenty-five."

Janice pushed herself up and joined the others.

Heidi closed the script and clasped it tight, eyes wide. "Whatever it is, it's surely a sign. The Marietta Murder Mystery Dinner Theater is going to be a huge success!"

Janice tried really, really hard not to meet Tess's gaze again. And though she failed, she was saved too many silent scoldings by the front door banging open.

"Move out of my way, Leila!"

Janice peered around Brad to see two young women entering, the older shoving the younger aside none too gently. Outrage marred her picture-perfect face.

Janice had already met Heidi's star actress and had wondered more than once if the young woman realized that being a drama queen wasn't a necessary qualification for someone who wanted to make a career upon the stage.

Dempsey Keller brandished a few pages of her own—crisp and white and new. "This had better be a joke! I will *not* just stand by and let all my best lines be cut."

Janice glanced at LuAnn, who wisely edged behind Heidi.

There was really something to be said for sticking to her sewing machine and hot glue gun. She'd happily leave dealing with cranky actresses to someone else.

CHAPTER TWO

"Only six orders? Really?"

Janice patted Heidi's arm and offered her a smile that she prayed looked encouraging and bolstering. They'd adjourned to the back patio to enjoy the warm spring evening while they waited for the rest of the crew to arrive. "You've still got nearly two weeks. But we just wanted you to know, so you can kick it into high gear."

Heidi sighed and sank onto one of the patio chairs. She pried free an escaped curl that had gotten stuck to her cheek, thanks to perspiration and makeup, and tucked it behind her ear. "Right. I've called the local radio stations and gotten in their announcements. And I have all those flyers and brochures that should be getting here any day. We'll get those around. And I've posted on my social media pages. What else should we do, girls?"

Janice followed Heidi's gaze to her two actresses. Dempsey stood at the bar-height table that went with their patio set, studying her nails and pouting. Leila sat on a stool, hunched over her phone.

"Well for starters, you could actually get your leading man here for a practice." Dempsey made a show of checking her watch and then frowned in the direction of the road. "I *would* like to rehearse sometime today. Even if I barely have any lines anymore."

"The paper's still going to do an article and photos, right?" Leila turned, phone held aloft, and snapped a picture of Dempsey.

Dempsey scowled. "Warn a girl before you do that. That's not my good side."

"Oh, come on, Dem, you don't have a not-good side." With a cheeky smile, Leila hunched again.

Dempsey grinned and fluffed her glossy dark hair.

Janice chuckled. The girls bickered like sisters sometimes. "Newspaper, radio, flyers, and brochures…that all sounds great to me. And if you all are waiting for Rand before you start rehearsing, we can do a few fittings in the meantime."

"Fabulous. This humidity's killing me." Dempsey sashayed toward the door.

Heidi waved them on. "You two go on in with Janice. I'm going to see if I can reach Rand and then dream about that script a little. Wouldn't it be cool if it was a genuine nineteenth-century murder mystery? Maybe we could adapt it and use it."

Janice grinned at her friend and cast a glance around the patio area. They hadn't opened this space to guests yet, but with the interior squared away, the last couple of weeks had seemed like a good time to work toward that goal. She, Tess, and LuAnn had spent last weekend getting the flower beds planted—much to the complaints of their backs. When they finished, the patio would make a lovely space for them or their guests to while away the evenings this summer.

But for now, it was apparently just what Heidi had been hoping to use for a setting in her production.

A production that Heidi's family, at least, would enjoy. Swallowing a sigh, Janice left her friend to her script and dreams and led the way back into the inn and up the stairs. Leila and Dempsey followed behind.

"You know what we need to start planning?" Dempsey said once they were on the stairs. "A cast party for after the show. A treat for Heidi, you know? Wouldn't that be fun? My granddad said we could use the back room at his restaurant for it."

"A cast party? For this sort of thing?" Leila sounded dubious. "I don't know, Dem. For a regular play, sure, I get it. But this seems different. If all goes according to plan, we'll have a new show every month. We can't do parties for all of them."

"So we call it a launch party. Whichever, I think it would be fun. You think so, don't you, Janice?"

Janice glanced over her shoulder at the young woman, who was pouting again. "I have to think Heidi would be very touched that you planned something like that for her, yes."

Leila shrugged. "Whatever. I'm sure if you want to do one, Dempsey, we'll do one." When a buzzing sound came from her phone, she lifted it again.

Janice wasn't sure she could trust Leila alone with her sewing machine, but she'd give credit where it was due—Leila could move her thumbs over that screen at lightning speed and still climb the steps without a stumble. If Janice tried that, she'd end up with stubbed toes and more autocorrected mumbo jumbo than intelligible words.

Dempsey jogged up a few steps to catch up with Janice. "So, my costume. I've been thinking, and I'm not sure I want blue after all. My character is supposed to be a mafia don's moll, right? I think I need something flashier. Red, maybe."

This was why Dempsey's costume was last on Janice's list. She bit back a laugh. "That was our original plan, if you recall. But you said it would be too overstated, and you wanted black. Which would be too funereal, so you wanted gold. Which would be too ostentatious, so you wanted blue."

"The character has been evolving in my mind as we rehearse." Dempsey made a circular motion with her hands, as if demonstrating the blossoming of her alter ego. "And with half my lines cut, I need a nonverbal way to make a statement." If she meant to cover her testiness, she failed.

But then, Janice doubted she'd really meant to. She reached over and patted Dempsey's arm. "Well, I have the lining done— you can try that on for fit and style, and then we'll make the final selection on fabric, okay? This is it though. When I say final, I mean it. I'll be ready to start work on it tomorrow, and once I cut, there's no changing your mind again."

"I totally understand." Dempsey clapped her hands together and did a little jig. "Oh! I love costumes! They are so the best part. Right, Leila?"

"Well—"

"I've been scouring those secondhand shops you told us about for accessories. That one run by the vintage chick has been amazing. I have a whole box of stuff in my car. Oh! I should have brought it in. Here." Spinning back to face downward, Dempsey shoved her script at Leila. "Carry that up for me, will you? And this." She shoved her small handbag at her too. "I'll be right back."

Janice opened her mouth to object, but Dempsey was already barreling down the stairs. And what was the point of objecting anyway? Janice had to get over her wariness of Leila. She said a silent prayer for the Lord's help with that.

Soon enough they were on the fourth floor, and Janice was switching on the light in her sewing room. Leila's costume still hung on the hanger she'd put it on an hour before, shimmering silver in the afternoon light. "There's yours, Leila. What do you think?"

"Just a sec." Leila made a few more swipes on her phone and then looked up as she tucked it into her pocket. Her eyes widened. "Whoa. That's seriously pretty, Mrs. Eastman."

"Try it on. Let's make sure it fits." Janice slipped it off the hanger and motioned to the bathroom attached to her suite.

When Leila disappeared into the bathroom, Janice turned back to her worktable. She still had the original red fabric Heidi had purchased for Dempsey's dress—they'd simply planned on making one of the audience costumes from it when Dempsey insisted she wanted something different. Janice had a rack of those costumes ready too—trickier, given that they had to be highly adjustable since they would be worn over other clothing. But it was all part of the experience.

17

Janice had made ten gowns for the women and collected an assortment of ties, vests, and fedoras for the men. Other accessories, such as feather boas and blinged-out necklaces, would be given to those who might not wish to be decked out in a full costume. Some of those would become clues as the night went on and the mystery unfolded. They'd gotten what they could from Antoinette's Closet for a song, but Heidi had wanted a few original costumes too.

Janice grinned as she ran a hand over the sequined red fabric. This dinner theater was going to be so much fun—she said a prayer then and there that it would be successful. Because it deserved to be, and because Heidi would be heartbroken if it wasn't.

The bathroom door swung open again, and Leila stepped out, her face wreathed in a smile as she ran a hand down her hip to smooth out the dress. "It's perfect! I can't believe you made this."

Janice smiled at the young woman's excitement. "It wasn't too hard a pattern. And it looks lovely on you—though I think it needs a few darts. Come over here, and I'll pin it."

Leila gathered her dark curls, twisted them up onto her head, and secured the mass with a ponytail holder as she walked. "It was so nice of you to do this for Mrs. Ingram. I think it'll really set her company apart, to look so professional."

Janice slid her strapped pincushion onto her wrist and motioned for Leila to turn her back. "It's been a pleasure to help out. I've missed creating costumes over the last couple of years." The extra money she was making from it might not really be enough for her time, but it was a joy. And Heidi was just getting started—Janice had insisted on cutting her friend a break on her rates.

Leila laughed. "Well if this goes like Mrs. Ingram hopes, she'll keep you busy. I still think she's a little nuts, to want to have so big a repertoire."

Janice had thought much the same thing when Heidi said she intended to roll out a new murder mystery every month for the first year to ensure customers could use the theater over and again without repeating a show. But who was she to tell her friend she was crazy? "If anyone can pull it off, it's Heidi Ingram." She gathered the excess fabric at Leila's waist and pinned it. "Raise your arms, straight out."

Leila obeyed, and Janice pinned the extra material under her arms as well.

As she was finishing up, Dempsey and Heidi came in, both carrying large shopping bags. Blue feathers spilled out of one, making Janice grin. Emma at Antoinette's Closet had obviously been at work.

Leila struck a pose for them. "Ta-da!"

"Oh, wow." Dempsey's eyes widened as she put her load down. "If yours looks that good, I can only imagine how gorgeous mine will be."

Janice tried to exchange a glance with Heidi, but her friend was setting her bags down with the other props they'd begun storing up here, and she didn't look up.

Leila rolled her eyes. "Did you get ahold of Rand?"

"He's running late." Heidi said it carefully, as if the words were glass and might shatter if she wasn't careful with them. "He should be here in about thirty minutes."

Dempsey shook her head and put on an expression of disdain. "And of course, he's picking up Luke and Scott, since Luke's car is still in the shop, so our guys will *all* be late. Again."

Which meant they likely wouldn't finish up their rehearsal until nearly nine o'clock. Janice sucked in a fortifying breath at the thought of the late night. The actors kept mostly to the café and away from the paying guests...until Heidi did something like send them out looking for good places to plant clues. They weren't disruptive, but even so, Janice, Tess, and LuAnn wouldn't close up for the night and retire to the fourth floor until they'd left.

But there wouldn't be many more late nights for this, one way or another. Janice gathered up the lining for Dempsey's costume and turned back around with a smile. "All right, Dempsey. Your turn."

Janice followed the sounds of her friends' voices into the office, sinking with a happy sigh into a chair. The rest of the actors had finally shown up, and she'd had them do a quick, two-minute fitting for the vests she'd made to go with their existing suits. Now she could truly call her work done for the day.

Tess looked up from the computer with a grin. "Ready to retire from stage and screen yet?"

Janice released an exaggerated sigh. "I don't know how Heidi keeps up with that crew. What are you all doing?"

"Trying to figure out what this is." LuAnn waved the faded blue script in the air. "Thus far, our internet searches haven't found anything, based on the lines we've put in."

"It's probably nothing. A local production that some hotel employee participated in, maybe. Could have stashed it in a book to keep from getting caught with it." Tess pursed her lips and scrolled through another page of search results. "Without a title to go on, it doesn't look like we're going to learn anything. Looks like this discovery's pretty much a bust, ladies."

LuAnn flipped through the pages again. "Ah, well. Not everything can be a hidden gem, I suppose."

"Can I see it?" Janice held out a hand to receive the brittle pages. Not that she had any greater insight than LuAnn into such things, but she'd yet to really get a close look at the script. Once LuAnn handed it over, she turned each page, looking more at the paper and layout than the actual words.

She frowned. "Is this typical for plays at the time? Some of it typed and some handwritten?"

LuAnn shrugged. "Keep in mind that if it was produced before typewriters, it would have been printed on a press. If there were lines that would change or be improvised, I guess it's possible they'd just leave those blank on the plates and let the actors fill them in."

"Interesting." Janice's gaze caught on one particular handwritten section. It had been underlined. Not uncommon, she supposed, if the script had belonged to an actor. He or she could have marked it up as they studied it. "Do we have any reason to think it's that old? I mean, it seems old, but..."

"There's a date on the back." Tess clicked something. "Or part of a date, anyway. We're operating on the assumption that's the date the play was published. Either that or when it was performed."

Janice flipped the script over and squinted at the faded writing on the back. It was in the corner, and part of said corner had been ripped off in a neat, straight diagonal line, as if it had first been folded and creased and then eventually torn. All she could make out was *0, 1851.* And then on the line below it, *lace.* She frowned. "Lace?"

"No idea." LuAnn ran a hand through her hair.

Janice pursed her lips. The words—or letters and numbers, anyway—didn't mean much beyond an indication of the year, but something else about them tickled the back of her mind. "Do you still have your copy of Prudence's journal down here, Tess?"

"Sure. But why? It doesn't start that early. The first entry is from 1856."

"I know, but...the handwriting looks familiar."

LuAnn frowned and leaned over Tess's arm to look at the script with her. "I don't know that there's really enough of a sample to tell whether it's a match or not."

"And I think a lot of old writing all looks the same. The way they were taught, I guess." But Tess dutifully fished out her copy of the journal written by Prudence Willard, a conductor of the Underground Railroad who had once worked at the inn when it was called the Riverfront House. They'd discovered the journal when they first bought the inn. She held it out to Janice.

"Thanks." Janice took it and flipped to an entry from 1861. She lined it up over the script, so the years were near each other. There was only a one-digit difference, and she hoped that would give them a pretty good idea of whether they were similar or not.

"Wow." LuAnn leaned closer. "I don't know about other people's writing looking the same, but these examples sure do to me. Not that I'm an expert."

Maybe not, but as an English teacher, LuAnn had seen plenty of examples over the years. All teachers learned to identify students by their handwriting because it was inevitable that a few would forget to put their names on their work. Even Janice had encountered that, and her classes had less paperwork than LuAnn's.

Tess rolled her chair over for a look too. "They do look alike. Isn't there an entry where she mentions how well someone crochets lace? We could compare that to the word *lace* on the script. See if she does that curlicue on the *c*. That seems pretty distinctive."

"That was from sometime in 1858, I believe." Janice flipped through the printout, her eyes tracking to the place on each page where she recalled seeing it. An avid crocheter herself, she'd taken special note of that.

It was a little surprising that Tess had, though, which made a grin tickle the corners of her mouth. Crafty things were not Tess Wallace's forte.

"There it is." Her gaze snagging on the reference to one of the escaped slave's talents with a hook and thread, Janice studied the word for a moment and then held the script next to it. "Same curlicue."

"Good instincts there, Janice." LuAnn nodded her agreement. "So we can probably assume the script was Prudence's. Or she had it at some point, anyway. Not sure what that really means though, or why she'd have put it in that book."

"Did the Mother Goose book have the Riverfront House stamp?" Janice lifted her brows Tess's way.

Tess shrugged. "I don't recall. Want me to check?"

"I don't know that it really matters. It would just be a little more evidence that it's Prudence's handwriting, since we know she's connected to the hotel." Janice flipped the printout closed and handed it back to Tess.

A knock sounded on the doorframe. "Hey there. Sorry to interrupt." Heidi poked her head in, smiling. "I think I've decided where I need to have the fog machine. Is it okay if I put it right up against the balcony railing, over the café? That way the fog will spill down from above, go down the stairs, and get the hallway there too. I can hide the plug under your runner."

"That sounds fine." LuAnn raised her eyebrows at Janice and Tess to make sure they agreed.

Janice nodded. "I don't imagine that would be in our way if you had it set up ahead of time." She leaned over to slide the script back onto Tess's desk.

"Ooh." Heidi stepped into the room, her gaze locked on it. "Figure out what it is yet?"

"Nope." Tess set it on top of the journal copy. "The internet knows nothing for once."

"Hmm." Heidi tilted her head, drumming her fingers against the doorframe. "My friend Keith might have an idea. He's studied a ton of nineteenth-century plays. I'll mention it to him, and I'll use the character names since there's no title."

Those were certainly distinctive. Janice had caught a glimpse of characters named Lulu Belle, Bean, Fiddle, and Kalamazoo.

"Sure." Tess lifted the script again and held it out toward Heidi. "Maybe snap a few pictures with your cell to send to him, if you want. Otherwise, we've got nothing."

Which would probably be what they ended up with anyway. In which case, they'd file it away with all the other random, interesting, but ultimately unimportant things they'd found at the inn and leave it at that.

Heidi pulled out her phone but then paused. "Oh, hey. The actual reason I came in was to ask for yet another favor. We were just talking about music, and I know you three are quite the vocal trio. Would you be open to singing something during the show? A live song could really be fun."

Janice clasped her hands together, knowing her eyes were wide with hope as she looked at her friends. She had a few books of twenties-era music, and already titles and possibilities were swimming through her mind.

Tess and LuAnn both took one look at her and started laughing. "I think that's a yes," LuAnn said.

Happy to leave the half script to her friends, Janice slipped out the door. "If you need me, I'll be at the piano!"

CHAPTER THREE

Thursday morning dawned clear, bright, and warm enough to hint at the summer soon to be upon them. Janice breathed it in, tilting her head back to better absorb the morning sunshine, and let her pace slacken a bit as she and her two best friends walked the riverfront. LuAnn, if left to her own devices, would keep them at a near-run. Janice much preferred a more leisurely pace, especially on a morning as beautiful as this.

The mist rose off the water in a curtain of silver and gold when the sun shot through it. Janice stood still and soaked in the moment. The scent of honeysuckle and dew, the kiss of cool fog and warming sun on her face, the chirping of birds serenading her. Mornings like this, it was easy to let words of praise swell to her lips.

"Wow. Look at that one." Tess had stopped a step beyond her and raised a hand to block the morning sun glinting off the water. Her gaze seemed to be fixed on a paddleboat lazily making its way toward the heart of Marietta. It was huge and gleamed white and gold.

"The *Gilded Palace II*." LuAnn squinted as she read the name, then let out a happy sigh. "Gorgeous. Can you just imagine taking a cruise on that a hundred years ago? I bet a few romances and betrayals played out on its decks."

Given the distant, dreamy look taking over her face, she was imagining a few now. Janice exchanged a grin with Tess and watched the sternwheeler for another minute, until it vanished behind the buildings of town.

Tess checked her watch. "We'd better get back to the inn. Marissa will be there soon."

Nodding, Janice did a one-eighty. To her way of thinking, it would have to be a slow news week for Marissa Endicott's special-interest piece on their first year of inn ownership to actually make it into the local paper. But it would be fun to do the interview and revisit the events of the past year, regardless.

It took her a few steps to realize LuAnn was still staring at where the boat had been. She laughed. "Hey, Walter Mitty! You coming?"

"Huh? Oh." LuAnn shook herself and hurried to catch up, her grin not even sheepish.

They walked in companionable silence for a few minutes, but then Tess started humming one of the songs they'd narrowed their choices down to last night. Janice grinned. This was going to be so much fun—it always was when the three of them got to perform, and this would be even better than usual. They'd all be in costume, and they'd get to help set the stage.

The song Tess was humming was Janice's favorite. She came in with the words on the chorus, smiling when Tess and LuAnn joined in too, filling out the harmony. "My Melancholy Baby" kept them company for the walk back, though their stroll became more challenging when they decided to add a few dance moves to it. They ended up dissolving into laughter by the time they let themselves in the back door of the inn.

Winnie greeted them in the kitchen with a shake of her head. "Living up to your motto, I see."

"Never be boring," Janice declared around a gasp for breath.

"And never act our age," Tess and LuAnn declared together, which resulted in another round of laughter.

Winnie chuckled too and turned back to the day's soups, already started on the stove. "You ladies need me to do anything beyond the ordinary today?"

"I don't think so." Tess brushed a strand of coppery hair away from her eyes and sucked in a breath. "With no one here last night, the rooms are still ready. We'll be half-full tonight, leading into the weekend though."

"And we have that interview this morning with the newspaper." LuAnn looked at the clock on the wall. "In fifteen minutes. I don't know about you two, but I think I'll run upstairs and freshen up."

Janice hadn't applied any makeup before their walk, so that seemed like a great idea to her too. She also changed into a prettier outfit and made it downstairs just as the bell over the front door jangled.

Tess had beaten her back down, apparently, and was emerging from behind the ornate bar they used as a front desk with her hospitality smile in place. "Marissa, hello! So nice to see you again."

LuAnn hurried down the stairs.

Janice moved forward, out of her friend's way, with a smile in place aimed at their visitor. "Good morning."

Marissa Endicott gave them all a smile. She was a lovely woman, probably in her early fifties, with a few smile lines around her eyes and mouth. Today she wore a stylish blouse in yellow, topped with a light jacket she'd probably have to lose in another hour or two. A camera bag was slung over her shoulder in lieu of a purse. "Morning, ladies. Thanks so much for meeting with me."

"Are you kidding?" Tess leaned on the bar. "It's our pleasure. We never argue with a little extra exposure to remind people we're here."

"Where would you like to talk?" LuAnn held out her arms. "The sitting room, the café? Or we could go outside."

Marissa nodded. "Outside, I think. It's a gorgeous day, and the light is great for some photos."

"Perfect." Janice motioned to the door.

"Then afterward maybe you could give me a tour, pointing out the restorations you've done." Marissa patted her camera case. "A few extra shots never hurt."

Janice held the door, and they exited back into the golden May sunshine. They circumnavigated the inn and ended up on the garden patio, everyone choosing a seat. A pleasant breeze blew through the garden, bringing the scents of spring flowers with it—along with a few whiffs of onion from the kitchen.

Marissa only sat long enough to free her camera from its bag, and then she was back on her feet with a grin. "Let me go ahead and get a few photos of you three, while the sun's where it is. The garden is the perfect backdrop."

Janice scooted her chair a bit closer to her friends' and leaned in, glad she'd chosen a simple, flattering black blouse. Glad, too, that her platinum curls had behaved themselves today. She smiled as Marissa's camera clicked, the woman shifting her position a few times and occasionally saying something to make them smile anew.

Janice was glad when the photo session was over, and she could relax. Marissa put the camera back in its bag and came up with a notebook instead.

Winnie chose that moment to appear, a tray in hand and a bright smile on her face. "Thought you ladies could use a few strawberry scones. One of our seasonal specialties," she said for Marissa's benefit. "I brought out a pot of the new Mocha Rocha tea we got in the other day too."

And this was why Janice favored slimming clothes. You just couldn't lose weight with Winnie Washington in your kitchen.

Marissa's eyes widened at the tray of treats. "Oh my goodness, those look delicious."

"And they taste even better," LuAnn assured her. "Winnie perfected the recipe for our guests over the weekend. Something to go along with her signature sweet rolls as different fruits come into season. Next she's going to do some blueberry lemon, I believe."

Winnie, in her element, handed a plate to each of them with a scone already sitting pretty as you please in the center. "I need to get back to my soup, but there's cream and sugar for the tea. Enjoy!"

She hurried back inside with their thanks following her.

Marissa had already sunk her teeth into her scone and laughed as a crumb dangled from it, making her hurry to catch it. "So good. Are these only available with breakfast, or during lunch too?"

"We make them fresh each morning, so if the customers happen to finish them off, that's that. But if there are any left, they go in our dessert case for the day." LuAnn, closest to the table, poured the tea.

Marissa licked some of the strawberry glaze off her finger. "Well, while I'm pigging out, why don't you guys tell me some of the discoveries you've made about this old place during your first year here. If I recall correctly from what Brad mentioned, the building has revealed a few secrets, right? In connection with the Underground Railroad."

"It seems like we discover something new every few weeks." LuAnn grinned and broke off a bite of her own scone. "Starting with the journal of a Quaker woman named Prudence Willard, who was apparently one of the people responsible for using Riverfront House—the hotel's original name—as a stop on the Underground Railroad."

"Then there was the quilt." Tess poured a dollop of cream into the cup of tea LuAnn had passed her.

"And the bones in the secret tunnel." Janice shivered at that particular memory.

LuAnn passed teacups to Marissa and Janice and then poured her own. "We've found jewelry hidden here, and clues that led us to an unpublished Mark Twain manuscript associated with the Willard family."

"And don't forget the soup recipe with a note for poisonous mushrooms. And the tunnels and secret ladders in general. And just yesterday, we found the script for a play seemingly hidden in a book, with Prudence Willard's handwriting on it." Janice added a spoonful of sugar to her cup.

Marissa frowned. "Didn't you just say she was Quaker?"

"That's right." Tess passed the cream to Marissa, who took it and added a bit to her cup.

"That's odd, then. From the research I've done on Quakers—I wrote an article about their presence in the Ohio valley a few years ago—they had a prohibition against the theater. Why would a Quaker woman have a play?"

Janice exchanged a look with LuAnn and Tess, but neither of them seemed to have any better idea than she did. "That could explain why it was hidden. Maybe she didn't want anyone to know she had it. It probably would have earned her a few frowns from the Friends back then."

Marissa granted that with a nod and opened her notebook with one hand while taking another bite of the scone she held in the other. After swallowing, she said, "Things have been pretty busy here over the last year, haven't they? Even having only been in town a few months, I've heard about quite a few interesting happenings. Can we touch on your purchase of the inn last June and the process of getting the place up and running?"

"Sure." LuAnn took the lead, detailing how they fell in love with the place but ran into a few snags as they looked into buying it, keeping it vague enough not to shed a bad light on the elderly aunts of Brad Grimes, who had tried to scare them away to protect ancient family history from coming to light.

But as her friends chatted about the highlights of the past year, Janice found her mind wandering to Prudence Willard instead, to the script, and to the question of why in the world she would risk censure from the Friends if it weren't an important document.

Janice knew about the burden of maintaining the good opinion of one's church. She'd never been part of a Quaker community, of course, but from what she knew of the Friends, they were a close-knit and strict group. They'd have expectations, and if a Friend didn't meet those...well, Janice had to imagine that it could result in being ostracized. Certainly in judgment. And disappointment.

She took a sip of her tea, letting the notes of butterscotch, coffee, and chocolate roll over her tongue. As blessed as she'd always been to belong to loving churches, they all had their bumps and issues and their failings when it came to forgiving what they deemed failures by their members. Surely it had been the same among the Quakers, or even more pronounced. And from all they'd learned about Prudence, she was a godly woman who valued her community of Friends.

Which brought her to the question Marissa had asked earlier: Why would Prudence have kept an unknown, title-less play? And what made it so important that she would risk judgment from the Friends for it?

Chapter Four

May 18, 1851

Prudence's hands paused on the butter churn when she heard the baritone voice on the porch. Her pulse may have increased a bit when she recognized the timbre, but she would never admit it. If she did, her friends would tease her mercilessly, and Anna Barton, her adoptive mother, would give her that chiding look and say, "Thee is too young, Prudence, for such interest in a grown man like Jason Willard."

He was only four years her elder. Not even a full four. Nineteen to her nearly sixteen. But Anna needn't worry.

Jason Willard didn't seem to notice she was alive anyway, other than in some abstract sense. She'd heard him a month ago refer to her as "the orphan Anna Barton took in." Though he surely only mentioned her at all because someone had asked who had baked the pie they were enjoying at the moment.

Still, she couldn't convince her arms to continue their up-and-down motion on the churn. Not with *him* on the porch, saying, "Good afternoon, Anna Barton. I wonder if I could impose upon thee for a few minutes? I find myself in sore need of advice."

Prudence forced air into her lungs with a long draft of a breath and turned on her hard, simple wooden chair until she could peep out the window. She could just make out his back. Work-worn trousers, still stained with the dirt of his fields. A cotton shirt that did little to hide his broad shoulders and strong back. Dark hair curling out from underneath his straw hat.

Anna chuckled, the sound drifting with the scent of lilacs through the open window. "Thee knows I always have time to dole out advice, Jason Willard. Sit, please. Would thee like a glass of lemonade? Prudence just made some this morning."

Prudence's fingers tightened around the churn's plunger. She'd just pulled bread from the oven too, and there was a cake in the larder. Perhaps Anna would invite Jason inside for a bite to eat.

"No," he said, the porch bench creaking as he settled onto it, leaving only the toes of his boots visible to Prudence. "Though I thank thee. I had best get to my point, because if thee cannot help me, there will be more work yet to be done today."

Anna chuckled again, even though she would have heard the serious note to his voice as readily as Prudence did. "Let me guess. Thee has need of another strong back for thy fields, and I am the first helper to spring to mind."

Jason laughed too, though it was short. Prudence could picture him lifting a brow at Anna's tiny, bent frame. "It is more thy wisdom I seek, actually."

"I am all surprise." Anna's voice smiled, as her lips no doubt did as well.

Prudence shook herself and resumed her work, pushing the plunger down into the churn and pulling it back up again. She'd been at it for half the morning already—the butter would soon be ready, and she couldn't leave the work unfinished now. But she was a deft enough hand that she made minimal noise at it. Not enough to drown out the voices from the porch unless they decided to whisper, though enough that those on the porch could probably hear it.

Her gaze darted to the open window again. Anna knew she was sitting right here—they'd been talking a few minutes before Jason Willard arrived. It wasn't eavesdropping, then, was it, when her presence was fully known by one party and could be easily discerned by the other?

Sometimes, even after years in this loving Quaker home, she still had a difficult time deciding what was sin and what wasn't. She wanted to obey God and her guardian. But some lines blurred, and the definition of *eavesdropping* was one of them.

Their guest was silent for a moment, and then Anna broke the silence. "Thee needn't hesitate on Prudence's account, my friend. She is discreet and loyal. Anything thee wishes to say to me can be said before her."

Prudence didn't know whether to smile or frown. Anna's faith in her and warm words demanded warmth in response...but only would have been spoken because of

Jason Willard's unspoken dubiousness in light of her presence.

She gripped the plunger more tightly and pushed it resolutely through the cream. Her arms were beginning to tire, which told her as clearly as peeking inside the churn would do that she was finished.

He cleared his throat. "If thee insists. But it is of a most sensitive nature. Thee is aware, I know, of my work with... well, with helping those less fortunate find better paths."

"Slaves, thee means." Anna's tone conveyed decisiveness. "Continuing the work of thy father—the very work that helped my Prudence find the freedom she'd been born to and then stripped of. Yes, I am aware."

Prudence's throat tightened. Sometimes the nightmares still haunted her. Being kidnapped from her home when she was only a child of eight, the shame as she'd watched money change hands for her and her parents. She would dream still of those years of labor, of the sharp rebuke of her mistress, of the yearning for freedom.

The Lord had delivered her after four years of that life, when her parents saw an opportunity for her to escape and had pushed her toward it. He'd given her a home here with Anna Barton. A community. Freedom again. But so many others were still in bondage, under cruel yokes.

Lifting the lid of the churn, she listened now for Jason's response.

He cleared his throat. "I felt the Lord calling me to this work years ago, when I was just a boy. I consider it an honor to continue Father's work now that he is gone. All of his work."

"I know he would be proud of thee."

He had felt a call upon his life when so young? Prudence peeked inside the churn, still now to offset the churning in her heart. She wanted to know. She wanted to know what the Lord had in store for her. If it was simply to support and care for Anna Barton in her old age, she wouldn't argue—the woman had given her a life, a home, an identity. It was a pleasure to do for her what her aging arms could no longer do for herself.

As Prudence's tired arms had told her, the cream had formed balls of butter, separated from the whey. The difficult part was finished. Now she had only to wash the butter, squeeze out any water or air, salt it, and put it in pats.

"I find myself in a difficult spot though," Jason said. "I have received a communication from our contact with details on helping two brothers cross the Ohio. But it is not in the normal fashion. Or rather, once they are across the river, it gets...tricky."

Anna made no response, though Prudence could well imagine the expression on her lined face—patience. Anna Barton was the master of patience. She would wait for hours for someone to get to the point, if need be.

Another lesson Prudence sometimes struggled with. If she were the one out there, she would be prodding Jason along with questions like, "And? How is it tricky?" But he obviously didn't need prodding. He'd come here seeking advice, after all.

Indeed, after a beat of silence, his voice floated through the window again, quiet and intense. "Arrangements have already been made for transportation to get these brothers to Canada. We must rendezvous with a sternwheeler. But I will need someone to receive the instructions from the boat owner while I am helping the brothers across the river."

"Thee needs suggestions from me?" Now Anna sounded incredulous. "But I know many of the Friends have helped thee and thy father before. Surely one will gladly help again."

"They cannot. Or will not." Frustration colored his voice. "The instructions will be given at a very specific time, in a very specific place, and none of the Friends will go there."

Prudence paused with her hand already deep in the churn to scoop out the butter. Where exactly had Jason Willard asked the Friends to go, that they would refuse?

Anna, again, didn't ask the question. She just waited.

Jason's sigh blustered in with the breeze. "It is a showboat. The instructions will be given during the performance. By the actors. Upon the stage."

He said each noun—*showboat, performance, actors, stage*— as if the words themselves were sinful.

"Hmm. I see now thy difficulty."

Prudence put the scoop of butter balls into the dish beside her on the table and reached in for more. Though her parents had been God-fearing, faithful people, they had not been Quakers. Sometimes the dictates of the Friends still felt strange to her—now, for instance. She had learned two years ago when she had asked to go to a local production of her mother's favorite play, *Much Ado About Nothing*, that the Friends shunned all theater as being a gateway to sin. Anna had patiently explained their reasons, that while such things had their roots in moral causes, the theater had degraded into senseless, often outright vile entertainment that led thoughts and deeds astray.

"I can find no one willing to venture into this den of sin, not among the Friends. And I am unsure who in Marietta itself I dare to trust. But I thought perhaps thee might, Anna Barton. I know thee is well respected by all."

Anna sighed. "William Holmes would not go? Or Hezekiah Stone?"

Silence followed, in which Prudence imagined Jason shaking his head.

She nearly mashed the butter in her hands. In general, the Quaker abstinence from the theater made good enough sense to Prudence. But in this particular case, when attending for an hour could save lives? She slapped the butter into the bowl before she could squeeze it to mush and dried her hands on her apron as she strode for the door. She pushed through it, coming out onto the porch between where Anna sat on the bench and Jason in the rocking chair.

"I will do it." She hadn't really thought about the words, or what they represented. Hadn't planned, when the day began, to volunteer for a mission to help escaping slaves.

But as she said the words, something smoothed out in her soul, something that had always been jagged, ever since she had stumbled, starving and exhausted, up these porch steps at the age of twelve. She'd been desperate for sanctuary, and Jason's own father, who had conducted her across the river, had promised her she would find it here with Anna.

Jason didn't even look at her. "I appreciate your willingness, Prudence Barton, but this is not the task for a child."

She expected a wave of embarrassment or even a surge of anger at being labeled a child. But instead, peace settled into that now-smooth place. Peace and certainty and a feeling she could only describe as right. "How old was thee, Jason Willard, when thee felt the Lord calling thee to this life? Did thee never help thy father with any small tasks when thee was sixteen?"

She was still seven months from sixteen, to be honest, but Jason wouldn't know that, and Anna didn't point it out.

He took to his feet, clearly ready to argue. But he looked at her, really looked at her, for perhaps the first time. "This is no small task."

She felt certain that incredulity shone on her face. "It is sitting in an audience for an hour or two, from the sounds of it. What could be smaller?"

His eyes, so deep and brown, sparked. "It is putting thyself in a den of iniquity. If thee thinks it small, that proves only how much a child thee still is."

Prudence glanced at Anna. She didn't want to overstep her adoptive mother's authority or make anyone question her tutelage and guidance with her—but she also couldn't let two slaves fail to reach safety solely because their escape involved the stage.

She found Anna suppressing a smile, her eyes gleaming. All the encouragement Prudence needed. She faced Jason again. "Perhaps it is because I was not born into a Quaker family, Jason Willard, but I cannot agree with thee. I have attended a play before, and I did not come out of it any worse than I was before. My parents enjoyed such things, and they were no less godly for it."

His eyes didn't soften any. "I will not cast aspersions on thy parents, whom I have never met. But our forebears came to these conclusions for good reason. Everyone knows that those who perform upon the stage are of loose morals. And that plays often glorify those loose morals."

"Everyone also knows that the Lord Himself ate with sinners. That He and His disciples frequently broke the laws of the Sabbath, when it was to do good. Does thee honestly believe He would not step into a theater for like purpose?"

"The Lord would, I think." His words emerged quiet and nearly mournful. "But that does not mean that we are all strong enough to do the same, without being sullied by sin. How does thee know thee is?"

She wrapped her hands in her damp apron. "I beg thee, Jason Willard, let me help. Let me do for others what thy father did for me."

For a long moment, he studied her. His gaze tangled in her gaze, his face revealing none of his thoughts. She didn't need to work to keep her spine straight or her eyes steady on his, to keep her chin at an angle both firm and respectful.

So many times since joining this community she had struggled to be what she ought. But not now. In this moment, the faith weighed easy upon her, her own convictions a rod of steel to lend her strength.

In that moment, she knew what all of Anna's whispers of encouragement, all her promises that the Lord had a plan for her, had pointed toward. This. Doing for others what John Willard had done for her. Breaking the laws of man to honor the laws of God.

At last, Jason looked beyond her. "Anna Barton? She is thy child. It is thy decision."

Anna laughed and stood to slip an arm around Prudence's waist. "She is my blessing. My daughter by love if not blood. But she is no child, Jason Willard. Why, I was planning my wedding when I was her age!" She gave Prudence an encouraging squeeze. "She is old enough and wise enough to decide for herself what risks she will take—to body and soul and heart."

Prudence's swallow stuck in her throat. She had assumed Anna would judge her too young. Perhaps instead she ought to have confided her heart long ago. She suspected this woman who had opened her family and home to her knew it anyway.

Anna's gnarled finger touched Prudence's chin, bidding her to look at that precious wizened face. "Is this what the Lord purposes for thee, my daughter?"

Prudence let the question seep in, let the answer well up, let the assurance fill her eyes. She nodded. "It is, my mother."

"Then thee has my blessing. And we have solved thy dilemma, Jason Willard. Thee has a new partner in thy work."

Prudence couldn't help but notice when she looked back at Jason that he appeared neither pleased nor relieved. Resigned, perhaps. And still wary. "Thee must be aware that thee will be risking more than the law, Prudence Barton, if thee does this. Precious few Friends know the details of this plan. They will see only that thee is disobeying the rules of thy faith. Thee will be judged for it."

She raised her chin. "Let them judge. I will stand sinless before God, which is what matters."

Was that a gleam of respect in his eyes? It was, she was sure of it. And it complemented perfectly the handsome smile he gave her. "So be it, then. I will come by tomorrow evening to tell thee all I know about thy task."

She nodded, as did Anna.

Jason nodded too, touching a finger to the brim of his hat. Then he turned to the porch steps and made it down them before pausing and turning back. "I thank thee, Prudence Barton. For standing up when no one else would."

She leaned into Anna's side, happy to borrow her mother's strength when her own knees went a bit weak. "It is what the Lord asks of me. Who am I to refuse Him?"

He smiled again, then strode away.

Anna chuckled once he was out of earshot. "Well, Daughter. It seems thee has finally landed on a way to get that young man's attention."

Prudence smiled. "And yet I wasn't trying."

"That is how thee can know it is attention worth having." Anna squeezed again and then stepped away. "Go. Tend thy butter. And think on all thee has committed to this day. The Lord's work, I think, will not end for thee after this one adventure."

Prudence watched Jason's retreating form for another moment—how long his strides were, what power he held in every motion. Who was she, a young woman barely out of short dresses, to be called to the same road as him?

And yet that conviction still echoed within her spirit. She could not know whether she would walk beside him for more than this one escapade. But she knew down to her bones that her feet would stay this path regardless. She turned with calm acceptance back to the house and the butter awaiting its wash and its salt. She would help Anna. Perhaps she would someday marry. She would do all a woman should for home and family.

But she would do more too, as the Lord led.

CHAPTER FIVE

Thank you all so much for taking the time out of your busy day to talk to me. I have no idea when they might run the article, but I'll be sure and give you a heads-up once it's scheduled."

Janice meandered back toward the front of the inn with her friends and their guest, raising a hand to shield her eyes from the late-morning sun as they rounded the corner of the building. As she'd predicted, Marissa had shed her cute blue jacket half an hour ago, and Janice was glad she herself had opted for capris when she changed after their walk. The day had warmed up beautifully.

"It was our pleasure." LuAnn had led their foursome on the tour through the inside of the inn for the last twenty minutes, pointing out all the interesting historical features and discoveries they had made, winding their way to the back patio again so Marissa could collect her jacket and camera bag and notebook.

"If you have any follow-up questions as you write, feel free to shoot me an email or give us a call," Tess said.

They all paused at the front, and Janice gave Marissa a hug. "I've been enjoying your articles since you came to town, Marissa. I can't wait to read this one."

"I can't wait to write it." Marissa smiled, making lines fan out from her eyes. "And I'll see if I can talk my best friend into coming to that murder mystery dinner with me. Sounds like fun."

Janice grinned. She'd be sure to tell Heidi that Tess had plugged the dinner theater quite enthusiastically during the interview. Maybe the article would come out before the show, and it would be mentioned. Couldn't hurt ticket sales, if so. "It's going to be a blast. We'll be performing a song too."

"I can buy the tickets online?"

Tess nodded, a gleam in her eye.

They said goodbye to Marissa, who strode toward the parking lot with a happy step.

"Well." LuAnn linked their arms together. "We plied her with scones and tea and told her all our best stories, and the inn was looking pristine. If that doesn't get us some good press, I don't know what will."

Janice and Tess laughed.

The inn's front door opened behind them, and a man stepped out, his gaze locking immediately onto Marissa's retreating form. A strange look passed over his face—one Janice would call concern if she could think of a reason for it. Did he know Marissa, maybe?

But he didn't trail after her. Instead, he turned to them, a smile eclipsing whatever worry had possessed him.

Tess shifted immediately into business mode. "Good morning. Can we help you?"

The man's smile lost traction again. "Hi. Yeah—or I came to help you, actually, but...sorry, I caught a bit of your conversation through the window. That was a reporter?"

The worry was back, in his tone as well as his face. Though why would this man be concerned about a journalist?

Tess's smile faded a bit too. "I beg your pardon?"

The man looked back to them and brightened again, though he still looked a bit wary. He was tall-ish, probably early forties, his hair dark and his skin tan. He held out a hand toward Tess to shake. "Sorry. I'm Heidi's friend. Keith. She said you'd found a script—but you, ah...you didn't mention it to that reporter, did you?"

LuAnn drew her brows together, clearly confused. "Why would it matter if we did?"

"Hopefully it doesn't." With a bit of a sheepish note to his grin now, he reached into his back pocket and pulled out his wallet. "I'd like to purchase it from you though. How much are you asking? Will you take fifty?"

"Oh. I...we..." Tess shot a wide-eyed glance at Janice and LuAnn. "We hadn't really considered selling it. And to be honest, I doubt you'd want it—it's in bad shape. We were just trying to figure out what it *is*, and Heidi said you might be able to help us with that."

"I might." He didn't put his wallet away, though he closed it. "But regardless, I'm interested in purchasing it, if you decide to sell. I have a collection—I pretty much just snatch up any historical scripts I can find, regardless."

Janice chuckled, knowing her smile looked dubious. "Even when it's only a partial? Of something so obscure? We couldn't find anything about it on the internet."

He darted one last glance at where Marissa was climbing into her car. "Doesn't much matter. I'm a collector of old scripts. The more obscure, the more I love them." He motioned with his wallet toward downtown. "I own an old-fashioned sternwheeler that I've refurbished to be a showboat. Nineteenth-century style. And we're performing nineteenth-century plays. I have a museum on board, and your script would make a great addition."

Janice nodded. "We'll certainly keep that in mind. I think we'd like to take some time to figure out if it's linked to the inn first though." She glanced at Tess and LuAnn to make sure they agreed with her. Both of them were nodding.

"Sure." Offering them a charming grin and an accompanying wink, he slid his wallet back into his pocket. "So long as I get first dibs. Did you want me to take a look at it now?"

"Oh." Tess made a face. Maybe her mind had gone to the list of morning chores they hadn't yet tackled, like Janice's had. "Yeah, okay."

"I can come back if later would be better." Keith motioned toward the waterfront. "I'm in town for a few weeks."

"Evening would probably be better." LuAnn, their resident schedule-lover and list-maker, narrowed her eyes in thought. "We're free after dinner tonight, aren't we, girls?"

Keith pursed his lips. "I'm afraid I have plans this evening, and our rehearsals start tomorrow for our first show this weekend.

But tell ya what." He pulled the wallet out again but this time just fished out a business card. "Give me a call or send me an email and let me know what times would be good for you. That work?"

Tess, being closest, took the card. "Sounds perfect. Thanks for understanding. Usually we'd have some time in the morning, but…"

"Hey, no problem." His smile was now worry-free, and he took a step back. "Nice to meet you all. I look forward to hearing from you."

They watched as he walked away, his pace steady, heading back in the direction of the river.

Once he'd rounded the corner, LuAnn chuckled. "In the words of one of my former students, 'Dude.' Did he really just offer us money for half a script? That man has more enthusiasm than wisdom, methinks."

The juxtaposition of *dude* and *methinks* set Janice to giggling. "Only you, Lu."

"Only me what?"

Tess was giggling too, neither of them able to give an explanation to LuAnn through their mirth. They wandered back into the inn. The phone was ringing on the front desk, and Janice picked it up. "Wayfarers Inn, this is Janice speaking. How may I help you?"

LuAnn motioned toward the café and kitchen and her tasks there. Tess moved into the office, no doubt to answer messages, leaving Janice to focus on the call.

After chatting with the woman on the line for a minute and making a reservation for her for the first weekend in

August, Janice disconnected and checked her watch. There was still a load of towels waiting to be folded in the basement, and her sewing machine was calling to her. She angled toward the office for a minute to let Tess know where she'd be.

Her gaze snagged on the old pages sitting on top of the file cabinet, creased with curiosity and mystery. Most likely it wasn't that important a find, but Keith's interest in it made her stare at it for a moment, tension in her neck. What if it *was* valuable? "Maybe we shouldn't leave this lying out." She stepped over and picked it up, letting her fingers brush the soft edges of the paper. "I mean, why do you think he was so concerned about us possibly having mentioned it to a reporter? Do you think he already has an idea what it is and doesn't want anyone else to get wind of it?"

Tess looked up from her computer. At first her expression was mystified, but then comprehension dawned. "Oh, the script. I don't know." Her brow creased. "Do you really think it's worth something?"

Janice shrugged. "I can't think it would be. But *he* kind of seemed to, didn't he?"

"Fifty dollars' worth, anyway." Tess stared at the pages for a moment, mouth set in a line. "Now that you mention it...I guess there's a possibility that he has an idea and wanted to buy it before *we* found out it was worth more."

Janice winced. "I can't think Heidi's friend would be a shyster like that." Or didn't *want* to think so. But...people were sometimes. She'd ask Heidi how well she knew him. If he was just a passing acquaintance whom she'd thought of because he was coming to town, then...

Well. Regardless, it didn't hurt to be careful with it. "Maybe we could put it in the filing cabinet. Or the safe."

Tess nodded and pulled out her inn key ring. She selected the small key for the filing cabinet. "I think this will be sufficient. It's not an original Shakespeare or anything, for sure." She fit the key, turned it, and opened the cabinet drawer.

Janice found a happy place in which to nestle the script and stepped back so Tess could close and lock the drawer again. A bit of the tension immediately left her. "I'm sure we're being silly, and he was just being nice. Or overeager."

"You're probably right." Though Tess still looked thoughtful as she turned back to her computer. "Except his concern with Marissa *was* odd."

"I'll ask Heidi about him next time we talk. In the meantime, I'm going to fold those towels, and then I'll head back to my sewing machine for a while."

"Sounds good." Tess clicked something on her computer, and a familiar page popped up, grabbing Janice's eye. The one for Heidi's ticket sales. Janice sighed when she saw no new additions to the total count. Tess cleared her throat but didn't point out the obvious. "I've got half a dozen emails to square away before the lunch rush."

"I'll be back down to help with that in about an hour. Let me know if you need me earlier."

With her friend's assurances following her, Janice made her way to the stairs. First the towels, then upstairs to the comforts of fabric and thread.

Voices drew Janice down the stairs that evening, a pile of costumes and a few props she'd been working on in hand. It had been her turn to cook dinner for herself, LuAnn, and Tess, and she'd just been putting the last dish away when the sound of the bell on the door jingling carried up the stairs. While her friends had come straight down to see if they could get the rehearsal underway promptly this evening, Janice had made a quick detour to her sewing room to grab the costumes and props she'd finished that afternoon.

When she reached the main floor, she had to sigh. Heidi, Dempsey, and Leila were there, and even Scott, the younger of the two college boys in the production. But no Rand. And no Luke.

Janice glanced at her watch. They were only five minutes late—at the moment—though if Rand's previous pattern held, that could stretch to an hour before he deigned to arrive.

Maybe that accounted for the irritation on Heidi's face. She was still dressed in her school clothes—a stylish, asymmetrical top in cool tones and crisp black slacks—and looked all the more intimidating for it as she glared at the door. "Well, we're not waiting for them again," she said as Janice gained the floor. Her hands were planted on her hips, and her long lashes swept angrily over her sparking eyes, then she turned them on the Inn Crowd. "Would two of you be willing to stand in for them? Hopefully by the time we get to the scenes where you have major speaking parts, they'll be here."

"Sure." Janice put her load down on a chair. The costumes were for Rand and Luke anyway, so there'd certainly be no trying them on just now.

"I'll help." LuAnn rubbed her hands together and grinned. "I'll take Rand's part. I always wanted to be a mafia don."

Janice laughed. "And I wouldn't mind being twenty-one again, so I'll be the son. No problem."

"All right." Heidi attempted a smile, but it still looked more irritated than anything. "Imagining this whole area is full of audience members milling about with glasses of punch and lemonade in hand, everyone work your way to your mark. LuAnn and Janice, you just stand here at the bottom of the stairs, glowering and looking intimidating. Oh, wait. Scripts." She pulled a few spares from the bag she'd tucked behind the front desk and handed them each a crisp, stapled stack. "There you go."

"Thanks." Janice opened hers to the first page and looked for any mention of Joe Jr., the character usually played by Luke. He didn't have many lines…and then he turned up dead at the beginning of the second act and became the mystery the guests would have to solve. "Though for the record, I'm not flipping over any railings like Luke does."

Heidi's tight smile failed to hide her frustration. "No? I thought that would be your favorite part."

"Right." Janice chuckled and looked over Luke's lines.

"Okay, let's get started. As a reminder, we'll explain the setup to guests as they come in, inviting them all to have a seat in the café at exactly seven o'clock. Dinner will be served while we play out Act One. Our cue to begin—"

"The music, yeah, yeah. We know." Dempsey rolled a hand through the air. "Let's just get going."

Heidi's lips thinned. "Let's not start out the evening being snippy, shall we?" She strode rather snippily over to her tablet, which she'd set up on the front desk with a portable speaker, and soon a moody twenties-era song was booming out, sans vocals.

Janice did her best to get in character, leaning against the banister while LuAnn stood a few steps up, looking out over the bottom floor of the inn as if she owned the joint, which wasn't a stretch. She did a great job of projecting the swagger of a mob boss, even while standing still.

As the song faded out, Heidi pointed to LuAnn, who, holding her script in front of her, said, "Who's that at the door?"

Janice followed along as Dempsey, Leila, and Scott all chimed in at the right times, none of them needing to consult their scripts. She had to give credit where it was due—they were a talented bunch. Dempsey sashayed into the café area with a cigarette holder in hand and a pout on her lips, believably delivering a flirtatious line to an empty chair as if a handsome man were sitting there. Leila rushed in, fully convincing in her put-on anxiety. And Scott looked genuinely bothered as he eased up to the stairs and delivered his line to Janice.

She checked the pages in her hand and cleared her throat. "Take it easy, Maxie, and go put your glad rags on. Ain't nobody gonna give us trouble tonight."

Janice knew she didn't pull off the twenties gangster slang very well, but Tess only laughed once, and LuAnn's nudge in her back seemed more encouraging than teasing. Maybe.

Yet another reason Janice preferred behind-the-stage work. Within fifteen minutes, they reached the end of the act.

The bell over the door jangled, and Rand and Luke blew in with the spring breeze. "Sorry we're late!"

The cheerful voice drew Janice's gaze to Rand Oberlin as he closed the door behind Luke. He was by all accounts an amiable man. His silver hair was threaded with a few remaining strands of dark, and a full mustache topped his ready smile. He'd done some rewiring for them at Christ Fellowship once, about a decade ago, and he'd done thorough, conscientious work. Janice had known his wife for ages and had always liked her.

But punctuality was not the Oberlins' strong suit any more than gangster-talk was Janice's, and Heidi took punctuality to a whole new level. She met the newcomers with a mighty frown and hands on her hips. "Half an hour, Rand. Again."

"Sorry." His smile didn't falter as he set a bag down where it would be in the way of anyone else coming in the door and shrugged out of the lightweight jacket that had his name embroidered on the chest. "Thought I'd get out on time, but..."

Heidi folded her arms. "Look, I know this isn't your day job. It isn't anyone's day job. But we're coming down to the wire here, and it's not okay that you miss half of our rehearsal time, when you know very well we won't have more than one more rehearsal here at the inn and that every hour we spend here is an imposition on our hostesses and their guests."

Janice gripped the script in her hands and shifted against the railing. She wished she and LuAnn and Tess could have given them more time to practice here, so they'd be able to find and recognize their marks. But they just couldn't have a troupe of players here when the inn was full. Frankly, they had felt a bit odd about letting them use the place tonight, when they were half-full. They'd consented only because this group of guests had let them know they would be out until ten. And there was only one other night before the show when the inn wouldn't be occupied.

Defensiveness overtook Rand's affability. "I said I was sorry, Heidi. What more do you want?"

"I want you to show up on *time*! That's what I want!" Heidi threw her hands into the air. "I want you to give a little respect to the fact that I've invested a lot of time and money into this, and I need it to succeed! I may not be able to control who comes to watch us or what they think, but I can make sure we do our best. And our best means showing up on time, learning our lines, and—"

"Hey." Rand spread his own arms wide. "You *begged* me to join this thing."

"Because you have presence and skill. But if it's not matched by dedication and discipline, then I'll find someone else. I don't want to. But I will. Last warning. And Luke—if your car's not fixed by tomorrow, you call *me* for a ride. Understood?"

If Janice wasn't mistaken, Luke was about to finish his second year of college. But he looked very much like the gangly high schooler she remembered loping down the hallways as he ducked his head and said, "Yes, ma'am."

"Good. Now turn to Act Two and take your places. We'll do Act One again *if* we have time." Fiery eyes moved to LuAnn and Janice and then flicked over to Tess as well. "Ladies, you're up at the piano."

The whole floor was saturated in silence, the air thick with frustration and tension. Janice felt as though she ought to tiptoe her way down the stairs and avoid everyone's eyes, but that was silly—*she* hadn't done anything wrong. Still, she scurried more than strode across the floor and toward the baby grand.

There would be a brief intermission between acts to give the diners a chance to finish their meals, and then they would be advised to take their clipboards in hand and be ready. The Inn Crowd would perform their musical number, and then the body would fall—Luke, performing his acrobatics to land safely on the floor.

LuAnn leaned close as they settled at the piano. "Better lighten the mood fast—we don't want any *real* dead bodies around here."

Never one to miss her cue, apparently, Dempsey's voice charged through the room to Janice's ears. "We can always do another rewrite, Heidi. Make it a mafia *princess* rather than a don running the show. Wouldn't that be a twist?"

A twist that would make Dempsey the star.

"Ha!" One of the boys—Janice wasn't sure which, but she thought it was Luke—laughed. "If you want to be the real star of the show, Dem, you can switch roles with me instead. We all know there wouldn't be a mystery to solve if it weren't for me."

Definitely Luke. His pronouncement brought a bit of laughter into his tone—and hopefully into the room.

Tess released a slow breath and rested a hand on top of the piano. "I'm not sure this group's even going to make it *to* the show, never mind ticket sales."

Janice pulled forward her sheet music for "My Melancholy Baby" from where it had gotten shuffled behind another book of music and pressed her lips together. She had already put dozens of hours into this thing—it wasn't going to fail if she had anything to say about it.

She glanced toward the doorway, knowing that if everyone was doing what they should, Leila and Scott should both be making their way into the room, which they were. But Leila once again had her phone out and held up.

Janice frowned, tensing. Surely Heidi would have something to say about that too, wouldn't she? In her current mood, she would surely not tolerate anyone being distracted by text messages.

Heidi, however, said nothing, so Janice turned her gaze back to the piano. With more gusto than the song really called for, she launched into the opening bars of the music.

CHAPTER SIX

Nana, look! Another bone!"

Janice held the fake gem in place until the hot glue had set and then dutifully turned to her grandson where he sat at the small table she'd set up for him. She'd found a dinosaur "excavation" kit a while back and brought it out for him on this drizzly Saturday morning. Seeing how hard the packed dirt was in the kit, she hadn't been too sure he would have the patience to chisel away at it. But he had been sitting there for an hour with the little scraper tool, and his enthusiasm didn't seem to be dimming.

Janice bent over to look at the piece of molded plastic peeking out of the dirt. "Look at that! Good job, Larry. What kind of dinosaur do you think it is?"

"I can't tell yet. I bet it's a giganotosaurus though. Or maybe a diplodocus."

Janice smothered a smile. She'd had the choice of T-rex, stegosaurus, or velociraptor when she bought the set, but her grandson was apparently far more imaginative than the creators of the toy. "Goodness gracious goat, sweetie, I don't think I can even pronounce those. What do they look like?"

"The giganotosaurus is really big, and it's one of the carnivore ones. Way bigger than a T-rex. That's why it has 'gigantic' in its name. I mean, sort of. And the diplodocus is a plant-eater. It's as big as the inn, maybe, and has a long tail. Oh!" His eyes lit up, and he lifted his chin. "Maybe it's a velociraptor! They're my favorite."

Janice chuckled and smoothed down a lock of his hair. Thank heaven she'd chosen the one she did. "Well, you keep digging up those bones, sweetheart, and then you can put it together. I'll show you the box if you want or—"

"No thanks. Real scientists don't have a box to tell them what they find. They've got to just put it together, so that's what I'm gonna do."

"Alrighty then." She leaned over to press a kiss to the top of his head. "You keep at it. I've got a bit more work to do here, and then we'll grab some lunch, okay?"

"Miss Winnie said she made macaroni."

Winnie did like to spoil him. "She did indeed, and it's ooey-gooey with cheese on top, just the way you like it."

Larry grinned and went back to his digging. There would no doubt be dust and crumbs of hardened dirt all over her floor by the time he was finished, but she had a vacuum and she knew how to use it. Besides, at this rate, it would keep him occupied until Stacy got here at three o'clock to pick him up. Score one for Nana.

She finished affixing the plastic gems to the cheap picture frame that would sit atop the mantel a week from today for the show. Inside would be one of the clues—a black-and-white photograph of Luke's unfortunate character, his father played by Rand, and Dempsey's character. Her watch told her those three should actually be here in about five minutes, assuming Rand was on time. They needed to take said picture, but they had to be in costume, and Janice had just finished up Dempsey's last night. The photo shoot would be done in the garden out back.

To her happy surprise, three distinct notes of laughter came up the stairs a mere seven minutes later, one of the tones actually belonging to Rand. On time. She smiled. Maybe Heidi's lecture actually had an effect.

Janice stood and glanced down at Larry to make sure he was still happily busy. He didn't even glance up from his scraper and slab of earth as the voices neared.

She poked her head out into the hallway just as the three actors came through the door at the top of the stairs. "Come on in, guys."

No, wait. *Four* actors. Leila trailed behind too, though she wasn't laughing with the rest of them.

Janice frowned. "Is Leila in the picture too? I still have to do the darts in her costume—I didn't think that was top priority."

"Huh?" Dempsey blinked at her and then looked back at Leila, as if she'd forgotten she was there. "Oh, no. She's just taking the pictures. Her phone has the best camera."

"Gotcha." Janice glanced at the phone in Leila's hand. It was in a pretty, bejeweled case—which reminded her that she hadn't unplugged the hot glue gun after her own bejeweling session. Waving them on, she ran back inside and took care of that before she forgot. A moment later the group sauntered in, earning a fleeting glance from Larry.

"Okay." Janice motioned to the three costumes she'd pulled off the rack first thing this morning. The red of Dempsey's dress certainly grabbed the eye and held it hostage. She suspected—hoped, prayed—the young woman would love that about it. "There you go, guys. You can take turns changing. Dempsey, why don't you go first? I can check and see if we need any adjustments. You're the only one who hasn't tried your costume on yet."

Dempsey's eyes held a gratifying sparkle as she stepped toward the dress, reaching out a hand to run down the satiny length. "Wow. Red was so the right call. This is gorgeous, Mrs. Eastman."

"Why, thank you. I imagine it'll look even better on, so shoo." Janice grinned and sent her glance past Luke to check on Larry again. She didn't think he would slip away while he had something as engrossing as dirt and tools and plastic bones in front of him, but she just never could tell with her little adventurer.

She was pleased to find him scratching away with the hook-shaped tool.

Dempsey spun toward the bathroom, dress in hand. Her hair, Janice noted, was already waved and pinned into a twenties style. She'd need a headpiece for the photo though. Where had Janice put that? Patting her pockets as if maybe she'd stuck it in there—as unlikely as that was—she turned in a circle, searching for the beaded, befeathered headband.

She spotted the red feather poking out of a mound of other accessories on her worktable and fished it out.

"Hey now, Leila, no photos yet. I'm not ready." Rand's voice was back to cheerful. Apparently the bad mood Heidi had plunged him into the other night hadn't stuck. Or it could just be that she wasn't here.

Janice turned around in time to see Leila lower her phone with a smile. "This is just to send to Heidi. To prove you were here on time."

While Luke laughed, Rand rolled his eyes. "I don't think she'd believe it even with visual proof."

"Man, did she ever chew you out." Luke picked up the hat sitting on the little wire shelf attached to the costume rack and practiced flipping it onto his head. "I'm surprised you didn't have teeth marks."

Rand tugged the brim of Luke's fedora down so it covered his eyes. "Watch yourself, pup."

"Get a watch, Pops."

Rand laughed. "That's Daddy-o to you."

Janice smiled at the easy banter and turned to the bathroom door just as it opened. Dempsey struck a pose in the doorway.

Luke obliged her with a whistle. "Lookin' good, Dem."

"Fits like a glove." She cleared the door and homed in on the headpiece. "I'm guessing that one's mine?"

"Yep." Janice handed it over. "There's a mirror on the door there, if you want to use that while the men get changed."

"Thanks."

Not surprisingly, the men were quick, and within a few minutes, the four were tromping down the stairs amid more laughter. Janice smiled as they left. As tense as things had felt on Thursday night, the group clearly got along most of the time. Though if they didn't hold up under pressure...

Janice pulled out Leila's dress, figuring she might as well put those darts in now. If she could get it finished while she was here, they could do one final fitting.

While turning from the rack to her sewing machine, her gaze flicked toward and out the window. It was another gorgeous spring day, and she couldn't resist stepping to the open window and breathing in the fragrant air just barely breezing through her screen. Movement below caught her eye.

A man was striding toward the inn. Nothing unusual there. But something about the dark hair and his way of moving made him seem familiar. She stared for a moment, trying to place him. When he turned onto their walkway, and she got a better view of him, it clicked. Keith. He was coming back, but hadn't they told him they'd email him when they had time to see him again? She was pretty sure Tess and LuAnn would have mentioned it if either one had contacted him.

Janice looked at Larry and did a quick calculation. LuAnn was running errands. Tess was helping Lizzie with the grand-kids today. Because they all had commitments, Robin was manning the front desk. Winnie was in the kitchen, the café servers ought to be there by now—it was by no means empty downstairs. Still, she ought to go and greet him, apologize for not getting in touch sooner.

Setting Leila's costume down, Janice moved to the door. "Hey, buddy, I need to run downstairs for just a minute and check on something. Are you okay up here?"

Larry speared her with a look he'd obviously picked up from his mother. The one that said, *Give me some credit, Nana.* "Of course."

She leveled a finger at him. It had been less than a year ago that he'd wandered off while the inn was still under construction and nearly given her a heart attack. And less than three months ago he'd repeated the stunt during the Valentine's festivities. The kid had a track record. "Do not leave this room, unless it's to step into that bathroom. Do you understand?"

"Sheesh, Nana, I'm not going anywhere. I'm working on this super-long bone."

"All right. I'll be back in a minute." He was six now, she reminded herself. He could be left unattended for five minutes in a safe environment. Still, that boy surprised her endlessly with his ability to find innocent mischief when she least expected it.

Janice hurried to the stairs, shooing Tom away from the door with a nudge, and went quickly down the first couple of flights. She was nearing the second floor when voices from the front desk reached her.

"I don't have any notes about that," Robin was saying. She had a perfect front-desk demeanor. Authoritative but friendly, firm but helpful.

"Oh, really?" Keith's voice sounded a little bit surprised, a little bit curious, a little bit put out. "That's odd. They said they'd leave it out for me to take a look. Could you take a quick peek around for it? It's got a blue binding but is missing the front cover and some of the first pages."

Janice's breath hitched. They hadn't described the script for him—though Heidi might have. Even so, what was he doing, claiming they'd left it out for him? None of them had spoken to him since Thursday. They certainly hadn't decided to turn the pages over to him. Was he trying to steal it?

Maybe not. Hopefully not. But he was lying, regardless, and that made the idea that the script was valuable look a bit more reasonable.

Janice waited one more minute to see what Robin might answer, and heard her say, "I'll just give Tess a quick call and see what she'd like me to do."

Keith's laugh sounded easy—he was apparently as talented an actor as Dempsey and Rand. "Oh, you don't have to bother her. I know she's busy today. She said she'd leave it in the office for me though."

Janice descended the final, grand sweep of the stairs. "No need to do that, Robin."

Keith stiffened and snapped his head her way. His smile faltered for a moment before regaining its place on his lips. "Oh, hi. I, uh . . . " He cleared his throat. "I just spoke to Tess on the phone a little while ago."

"No you didn't." On the main floor, Janice advanced and rested a hand on the smooth top of the bar. She said no more. She didn't have to.

Keith shoved his hands in his pockets. "Just a few minutes ago."

"If it was just a few minutes ago, how would she have left it out for you? She's been gone for hours." She sighed and met his gaze, holding it for a moment. Long enough to make it clear she saw right through whatever this was. Keith backed up a step—maybe his own guilt was propelling him, or maybe he just wanted to make a quick escape. "Look, I'm not trying to cause any trouble. I'm just dying of curiosity here. Can't you just show it to me? I won't even touch it. I just want to see it."

Janice tilted her head to study him from a new angle. What was she to make of this guy? He didn't strike her as dangerous or the sort with larceny in his heart, but how was she to be sure? Regardless, he'd come here with some underhanded intentions. And she wasn't going to make any decisions about the script without Tess and LuAnn. "Look, Keith, I appreciate your enthusiasm, and I'm sorry we haven't decided on a time yet for you to see the script, but this?" She waved a hand at him and Robin. "Do you really think this is the best way to do things?"

Keith blew a loud breath through his lips, at least having the decency to look sheepish. He rubbed a hand over the back of his neck. "I'm sorry. I'm just…desperate."

"But why? It's just a ratty old partial script."

A sad smile curled up one side of his mouth but seemed to forget to tug the other up to match. "Would it endear me to you if I told you it was for love?"

She blinked at him. "Come again?"

He shook his head and moved to the door. "Never mind. Again, I'm sorry. This was a stupid idea, and rude of me. I realize I've probably ruined everything now, but…if you change your mind?"

Having no idea what to offer in response, Janice made none. Just stood there beside Robin, her mouth ajar, and watched him leave.

When the door closed behind him, Robin leaned close. "What was that?"

"I have no idea." Janice shook herself and looked upward, praying Larry was still where he belonged. "But I can't stand around trying to figure it out while my little adventurer is up there." She took one step toward the stairs and then stopped, looking over her shoulder at Robin. "Hey, if he comes back, let me know, okay?"

"Of course."

Janice turned toward the stairs again, but well-ordered color nabbed her attention from the edge of the front desk. A stack of brochures for the murder mystery dinner theater—those didn't surprise her. Heidi had said she would send some for them to hand out. One of the actors must have brought them along and deposited them here as promised.

But it was the second stack that raised an eyebrow. She picked up one and frowned at it. *Showboat!* it declared in a fancy, Victorian-style script. *Enjoy an evening on the river and be entertained in style!*

The photograph on the front of the trifold brochure was the paddleboat they'd seen the other day. The *Gilded Palace II*. What were these doing here? She flipped it open, her eyes skimming over the snapshots of stages filled with actors, artifacts in glass cases, and a schedule of summer shows. Her gaze settled at the photo of a dark-haired man grinning up from the back corner. Owner and director, it said. Keith Johnson.

He'd brought his brochures here, when he'd come to snoop and maybe even steal? Wow. That took some nerve. Shaking her head, she stashed the stack behind the desk to show to Tess and LuAnn later.

She found Larry right where she'd left him and dug up a smile for him. "Ready for your lunch break yet, kiddo?"

He eyed the dinosaur dig—he had four bones out now—pursed his lips, and tilted his head before nodding. "Yeah, I guess now's good. I'm kinda hungry. And I wanna look at my dinosaur book for a while."

And she could use a few minutes to reset her brain before she got back to work. "All right, come on then. Miss Winnie sent your macaroni up here for you—it's in the fridge. And we have brownies for dessert."

While she was warming up the cheesy pasta for Larry and scrounging up a fruit cup to go along with it, the four laughing actors came back up the stairs, heading straight for her rooms. So much for getting those darts in while they were here. She moved into the hallway so she could call out, "Just hang the costumes back up, guys. I'm here in the kitchen if you need me."

"Okay!" one of the girls shouted. Dempsey, she thought.

The microwave beeped. Janice set the fruit cup on the table on her way to retrieve the warm pasta. She added a fork, napkin, and cup of water to the place before Larry, then peeked out into the hallway to try to hear what the crew was up to.

"You can get back to work if you have to, Nana," Larry said around a bite of macaroni. He flipped *The Ultimate Dinopedia* open. "I'll just look at this while I eat."

She knew for a fact that's how he spent many a lunchtime on days when he was home, and that Stacy was usually getting chores done while he was thus occupied. "Okay. I'll come check on you in a few minutes to see if you're ready for your brownie."

"'Kay." He was already engrossed in the pages.

Janice scurried out of the kitchen, nearly tripping over Tom, who was trying to make a dash for the door the actors hadn't totally shut behind them. With a sigh, she scooped up the cat and nudged the door closed in a single motion. "Oh no you don't, Mr. Sawyer. Last time you escaped, you made a guest go into a fit of eye-watering and sneezing. You just go find yourself a nice patch of sunshine and take a nap."

Tom's answer was a meow and friendly head rub against her chin before he lunged toward the ground. She let him go, and he galloped straight down the hall to LuAnn's sitting room. His favorite spot—other than the top of the bookshelves downstairs, where he wasn't supposed to be.

Janice employed a more sedate pace toward her own sitting room and sidestepped Rand once inside so she could take her seat at her sewing machine. Although the moment she sat down, she frowned. The spool of red thread she'd still had on there from Dempsey's dress was missing from the pin on top of the machine. She knew very well she'd left it there, because she'd snipped a length of it off that morning to secure a loose sequin on the headband.

"Where in the world...?" She checked all around her table, under the stack of props, and eventually thought to crouch down and check on the floor. She finally spotted the thin trail of red and followed it under the costume rack, where the spool had rolled to a rest against the wall. Maybe the cat had been playing with it again—it wouldn't be the first time.

"You need any help, Mrs. Eastman?" Luke asked from somewhere above her.

Janice reached under the rack, nabbed the wayward spool, and then held out a hand. "Wouldn't turn down a hand up, but otherwise I've got it."

The young man obliged with a grin, and Janice turned back to her machine. But her frown only deepened. The thread wasn't the only thing missing. Where on earth was the foot pedal? Someone had unplugged it—and without that, the machine was useless. "Goodness gracious goat!"

"What?" Dempsey emerged from the bathroom, dress in hand and amusement on her lips. "Did you say *goat*?"

Janice pressed a hand to her forehead. "Where in the world is the foot pedal?" The cat certainly wasn't responsible for that going missing. Though who was, she couldn't imagine. It wouldn't have been Larry—he was around her sewing machine all the time and never bothered it.

But why would anyone else mess with it? She turned to look at the collection of actors. "A foot pedal with a cable that plugs into the sewing machine? Anyone see it?"

They all looked clueless. But then, they were all actors, so it was hard to gauge their true feelings.

No, that was silly. What reason would one of these four have for taking, of all things, a sewing machine pedal?

But they were the only other ones who'd been up here, and Janice certainly hadn't done anything with it. Her gaze swept over Leila and paused. She didn't have any proof she'd been the one to tamper with those machines in her classroom. But if she had...was she tampering with this one too? Why?

"We'll help you look." Dempsey's smile shifted from amused to encouraging. She hung her dress back up and promptly spun to peer into a corner.

"Right." Luke headed toward the opposite corner. Rand assigned himself to the pile of props and started sorting through them.

Leila put her phone down and started poking through a box of fabric and other supplies by the sewing table.

Janice didn't want to assume. Didn't want to cast blame where it didn't belong. But her neck tightened as those old suspicions clawed their way into her mind again. She spun in a slow circle, her eyes alert for anything else out of place. Everything looked normal. A collection of fabric and sequins, stray glitter clinging here and there on her worktable and the floor under it, assorted notions crowding the table.

It was such a strange thing to go wrong. She knew well she couldn't have moved it by accident—she never unplugged the pedal unless she was moving the whole machine, which she hadn't done in months. The animals couldn't have done it. It had to have been a person, and it had to have been intentional.

"Is this it?" Dempsey bent over and pulled up the familiar thick gray cord.

Janice moved over to follow it down. The pedal had been lodged between the box and the wall. It came out easily enough, but why on earth was it there? "Yeah, this is it. Thanks." Even to her own ears, her voice didn't sound exactly relieved. Not with all the questions still ricocheting.

Dempsey tugged it out and handed it over.

Janice plugged it back in and then opened her box of thread. At least the spool of gray for Leila's costume was where she had left it, along with the full bobbin spool. It ought to be enough for the darts. She opened the bobbin compartment and slid off the red, put it in the box with the big spool, and loaded the new color into place.

Leila didn't move, other than to lift her phone. "Do you mind if I record you working for a minute or two? I'm making a video of the behind-the-scenes stuff."

She should go and check on Larry in a minute. After she got the needle threaded with gray. "I guess that's fine. It's not exactly reality show stuff, and I'm certainly no super-model hostess, but knock yourself out. In a minute. First I have to check on my grandson."

It only took her a few seconds to pull the thread through the take-up and guide, poke it through the needle, and position it at the back. She'd catch the loop from the bobbin in a minute. Assuming no one took it from her machine in the thirty seconds she'd be away from it.

"Cool. Thanks." Leila pointed the phone at the guys. She certainly didn't seem to be experiencing any guilt. But did that mean she hadn't done anything wrong? "Give me a hat-flip, Luke."

While Luke tossed the fedora toward his head again— toward, but not onto, which earned the laughter of the others—Janice slipped back out to the hall. Her nerves were in full fluster-mode. First Keith, then the missing thread and foot pedal. She paused for a moment in the hall to close her eyes and say a silent prayer for clarity and peace. Breathing in deeply, she then opened her eyes and continued to the kitchen.

"Hey, Nana." Larry's bowl was nearly empty, and he looked up at her with big eyes behind his glasses. "Could I have some chocolate milk with my brownie, do you think?"

"Oh, I think the brownie is chocolate enough, baby. But you can have some plain milk. You done with the macaroni?" At his nod, she cleared the bowl and the empty fruit cup away. After sneaking the last two bites of pasta into her own mouth— you just couldn't let Winnie's mac and cheese go to waste—she poured some milk, slid a brownie onto a plate, and put both in front of him. "Are you going to keep reading or come back to digging when you're finished?"

He flipped another page, to a Utahraptor—one she could actually pronounce! He traced a finger along the drawing of one of its vicious-looking claws. "I'll just look at this one while I finish eating. Then digging." He glanced up with a grin. "And I'll go straight there, I promise."

Well, she knew when she wasn't needed. She headed back to her sewing room, where the older three looked ready to go.

"We'll get out of your hair, Janice," Rand proclaimed the moment she entered the room. He smiled and motioned the other two toward the door. "Thanks again for letting us drop in today."

"No problem." She stood aside so they could pass and then stepped into the doorway behind them. "Hey, could you be sure to close the door at the top of the stairs behind you? We have an escape artist of a cat."

Rand laughed. "Will do."

It wasn't that she didn't believe him, but she still waited until the door clicked behind them before she turned back to her sewing machine. And to Leila, who stood with her phone at the ready and an accommodating smile on her lips.

"Just ignore me," she said. "I won't bug you, I just want a few minutes of you doing your thing."

Janice returned her smile and obliged. She sat, caught the bobbin thread, grabbed the silver dress, and got to work.

Putting a few darts in only took a couple of minutes. Even so, she was surprised to find Leila hadn't left already by the time she was done. She surely didn't need that much video. Why was she lingering? Janice lifted her brows. "Did you want to try it on again?"

"No, I just..." Leila took a step back. Her smile had shifted into sheepish. "You make it look so easy."

Janice snipped the thread, her mind traveling back three years to those two weeks Leila had been in her class. She'd been behind with every step, and it hadn't come as a great surprise when she dropped the class—it was also why she'd led the suspect list when the machines were sabotaged. During her last day in class, she hadn't just been disheartened, she'd been clearly frustrated.

No frustration remained now. She seemed, if anything, yearning. But was that real or a show? Janice drew in a breath and tried to figure out how to respond. Before she could manage it, though, Larry barreled into the room chanting, "Let me at those bones!" with every step.

Janice dug up a smile and held it until the doorway was empty again. She just didn't know what to make of that girl.

CHAPTER SEVEN

"There we go." Tess secured the freshly snipped article from the newspaper under one of the anchoring ribbons on the bulletin board in the office.

Janice stood elbow-to-elbow with her and LuAnn and looked at it with a smile. Marissa had written a beautiful article that did a fabulous job of capturing the charm and history of the inn and the challenges and victories of owning it. And it must have been a slow news weekend, because it had made the front of the Regional section in yesterday's Sunday edition. Not exactly *the* front page, but they'd take it. None of them could believe it when they saw that not only had Marissa finished it already, but that it had been printed.

"We ought to get a frame." LuAnn regarded the pretty bulletin board with its crisscrossing ribbons—to avoid putting holes in things—with a smile. "That takes up half your board, Tess."

"We should. How big a one will we need?" Tess asked.

"I'll get my measuring tape. I left it on the front desk." Janice spun out of the cheerful office and took the few steps to the reception desk. A slew of weekend guests had just finished checking out, and café customers would likely begin arriving in about half an hour, but right now they were in the lovely midmorning lull. Also known as the few minutes between cleaning up after breakfast and needing to get to work on the newly vacated rooms.

Janice scooped up the coil of her cloth measuring tape, then halted when the phone rang. She picked it up with a cheerful, "Wayfarers Inn. This is Janice, how can I help you?"

"Hello. Is this Janice Eastman, one of the owners?" It was a woman—one with a honeyed Southern accent. The refined kind that always said Old Virginia to Janice's ear. Though she had no idea if it was or not. Could be New Georgia for all she knew. But it wasn't the Ohio version of Southern, that was for sure.

"That's right." Most people these days looked them up online before they called—in fact, most made their reservations online—so it was no surprise that the caller recognized her name.

"This is Bella Jasper with the *Columbus Dispatch*. I just read the article Ms. Endicott wrote about your inn and thought I'd call with a few questions of my own. Do you have a minute?"

Janice plunked the measuring tape right back down on the counter and plunked herself right down on the stool. "Of course I do." Coverage in a bigger paper would mean much more exposure and could only be good news for them.

"Great. I'm particularly interested in the things you've discovered that are related to the Underground Railroad. How about we start with the most recent find that Marissa mentioned—the script? What can you tell me about that and its ties to the UR?"

The hairs on the back of Janice's neck rose up a bit. "Not much. We don't have anything to suggest it even was tied to the freedom work." And the article hadn't said it was either. She'd just reread it not fifteen minutes ago, while they were talking about what to do with it. All it said about the script was that they'd recently found an unidentified one in a box of Riverfront House's books. Marissa had framed it as a mystery, not as anything related to the Underground Railroad. It was possible that this Bella Jasper had misunderstood. It had been mentioned in the same paragraph as some of their other finds that definitely were tied to the railroad. She drew in a deep breath and told her neck hairs to relax. "Sorry there's nothing more to share about that. It's really just some paper we found in a box of books. That's it." She could mention the handwriting on the back…but didn't. Marissa hadn't mentioned it in her article, and Janice had no desire to do so for this woman on the phone either. "But we have plenty of other finds that we know are related to either conductors or passengers on the Underground Rail—"

"Wonderful." Her tone, however, sounded frustrated. "I would love to hear about them, but I have another call coming in. Can I call you back in a little bit? This number good?"

Another call could account for the frustration, Janice supposed. She smiled to try to inject some ease into her own voice. "That's fine."

"Thanks so much. Bye-bye."

After hitting the End button on the phone, Janice stared at it for a moment.

"Who was that?" LuAnn moved up behind her and picked up the measuring tape.

Janice pursed her lips. "A reporter with the Columbus paper. Asked about the script and its ties to the Underground Railroad, then had to get off mighty quickly when I said it had nothing to do with it that we know of." She turned to the computer. Maybe she was just being suspicious, but those little hairs on the back of her neck wouldn't stand down. She wiggled the mouse to bring the screen back to life and clicked into a search browser.

LuAnn leaned on the desk. "Something strike you as not right?"

"Maybe." She searched for the *Columbus Dispatch* and scrolled through their site for a few moments before finding the staff directory at the bottom of the page. A click on that, and she was scrolling down through the list of all the staff writers and managers and their contact information. There, under Features, she found the name she was looking for.

Bella Jasper. She really was a writer for the *Dispatch*, so Janice should probably just relax. Instead, she pressed the button on the phone that paged through the caller ID. Glancing down at the first number and then at the one provided in the directory, she narrowed her eyes. "Not the same number."

"That doesn't mean anything in this day and age. She probably has a phone at the office, but she could have called from her cell." LuAnn straightened again. "Though if she raised your suspicions, just shoot her an email or call the number there and ask her any questions you want to ask her."

She should probably just let it drop and follow LuAnn back into the office. What did it really matter, after all? And she probably wouldn't have thought twice about it had this Bella Jasper not asked about the same thing that Keith of the *Gilded Palace II* had tried to sneak access to.

Neither Tess nor LuAnn had known what to make of that when she told them about it on Saturday night. Had he really just wanted a glimpse of it? Would he have tried to steal it? And for goodness' sake, why? He'd mentioned love, but that hadn't made any sense to them either.

Sucking in a breath, Janice dialed the number provided by the website. If Ms. Jasper had called on her cell phone and wasn't at her desk at all, then she'd have to decide whether to leave a message or not.

"Hello, this is Bella Jasper. What can I do for you?"

Janice blinked at the crisp, clipped words. "Oh. Hi." What had happened to the Old Virginia accent? For that matter, this woman's voice was a few notes higher too. She cleared her throat. "My name is Janice Eastman, part owner of a historic inn down in Marietta. This might sound strange, but…did you just call me for an interview? Or have an assistant or something call?"

The woman barked out a laugh. "Assistant? I wish. And no, I haven't called. Should I have?" Curiosity took her voice up another half step.

Janice couldn't help but laugh. "Absolutely you should have. We're a beautiful inn in Marietta with ties to the Underground Railroad." Might as well plug where she could, right? "Our local paper just did a feature, and I spoke with someone a few minutes ago from a Columbus paper who said she'd read it. Perhaps I misheard the name."

Or perhaps "Miss Old Virginia" had lied.

Again, though, why?

"Interesting. Just a sec." The sound of tapping keys came through the phone. "Marietta...so are you Wayfarers?"

"That's us."

"Cute place. I didn't call, but I'll do some research, and you might hear from me next week. I don't know who else would have gotten in touch with you from our office, but I'll check around. And if it was someone from another paper, I'm happy to beat them to the punch." She chuckled. "*Is* there a punch? Do you guys have something interesting going on?"

Janice smiled at the computer screen. "Always. Why, we have a murder scheduled for this weekend."

A beat of silence. Surely there was some kind of award for rendering a reporter speechless. "Pardon?"

Janice laughed. "We're hosting a murder mystery dinner theater on Saturday."

"Oh." The woman's voice rang with laughter again. "You got me. Good one. Could you give me your name again? I'm going to jot it down."

Janice provided her name and the inn's number and then disconnected. She would probably never actually hear from the real Bella Jasper again...but then, lining up an interview with the Columbus paper hadn't been her goal.

She tapped her fingertips on the smooth, deep wood of the desk and then turned back to the office, leaning into the doorframe. "So that was odd." She quickly brought her friends up to speed.

Tess let loose a burst of laughter at the "scheduled murder" bit. "You didn't!"

Janice wiggled her eyebrows. "Our grandkids aren't the only ones with mischief in them."

LuAnn laughed too, but then tilted her head. "Did you try looking up the number that did call?"

"No. Not yet." But it only took a few seconds to grab the cordless handset and read off the number to Tess, who was stationed at her computer.

She shook her head. "It just says, 'This call was located in the United States. The area code is Pittsburgh.'"

LuAnn hummed and leaned against the wall. "Do you think it has anything to do with the showboat guy? He could have put someone up to it. He's the only person I know of who would be so interested in the script."

Janice shrugged. "I don't know. It's possible. Can you hand me his card, Tess? I'll give him a call."

"Sure." She pulled forward the Rolodex of business cards and flipped through for a minute.

Janice punched in the number that Tess read off and put the handset on speaker so they could all hear it.

"Hello, *Gilded Palace II*, this is Keith speaking."

Definitely Keith's voice. Not that she'd expected anything different. "Hi. This is Janice, from the inn." Now, how to go about this delicately? "Did you just have someone call us, trying to find out more about that script? One of your actresses, maybe?"

Okay, so that wasn't exactly delicate.

"Better not have been. My actresses have been in rehearsal all day—we open this weekend, you know."

Really? The same weekend as Heidi's show? Maybe it was no wonder, then, that their reservations had been low. After all, the showboat looked to be a bit bigger of a deal than the six-person show that was Marietta Murder Mystery Dinner Theater.

"Why?" Dread darkened the guy's voice. "Who called? What did she ask?"

Was he acting? He didn't sound like it. But it was still possible that it was one of his actresses, wasn't it? Someone who'd heard of his frustration trying to find something out and had decided to try her hand at helping? It would have been a simple matter to look up a writer from an in-state but not-local paper and use the name. Try to get some information to make her boss happy. And did anyone really have an accent like that? She should have thought "actress" from the start. "I don't know who it was. A woman. She claimed to be a reporter with a Columbus paper, but I called the paper, and it wasn't her. The woman who called asked about the script's ties to the Underground Railroad, and when I said we had no evidence of any, she ended the call."

Keith sighed into the phone. "Did you tell her anything?"

Janice glanced up at her friends, who were both watching the phone, as if they could get a read on the person on the other end by visually dissecting the handset. "Well, given that there's nothing to tell..."

"Right. What did she sound like?"

Janice frowned. "Southern, female. Not sure how else to describe her."

Another long sigh, followed by a mumbled, "Theresa."

"You know who it was?"

The sound of shuffling papers came through the phone. "Maybe. I'll see what I can find out and get back to you, if that's okay. And, um...if I could ask you not to say anything about it to anyone else until then? I know that's asking a lot, but if it *is* Theresa..."

LuAnn straightened. "Why, who is she? Is she dangerous or something?"

A dry laugh came through the line. "Only to me."

Janice opened her mouth to ask for more information, but a click sounded, and the phone's display showed the call had ended.

Janice looked up at her friends. "Well? What do you think?"

Tess spun back around to her computer. "I think while Keith is doing his digging, we ought to do some of our own."

"We have been," LuAnn pointed out. "We haven't found anything."

"About the script, no. But maybe it's time we look at this thing from a different angle." Tess looked toward the office.

Janice exchanged a look with LuAnn.

"What angle?" LuAnn asked.

Tess lifted her brows. "The *Gilded Palace* and its owner. Maybe we should do some research on Keith and his business."

Janice wasn't so sure that would help solve the mystery of the script—but if it could shed any light on their new acquaintance and his behavior, it sounded like a fine idea to her.

May 20, 1851

"Thee is out of thy mind, Prudence Barton!"

Prudence ignored her friend's chiding and continued on her path, her eyes set on the long line of people waiting to purchase a ticket for the showboat sitting at anchor. The *Gilded Palace*, it was called. Her gaze traced the ornate lettering on the large boat, the fresh white paint under it. Even from here, she could hear the music spilling from its decks. The laughter. She could see the citizens of Marietta decked out in their finest under the boat's lamps.

Gilded, indeed. A stark contrast to the simple life she'd come to love under Anna Barton's tutelage. This reminded her of something far different. The only time in her life she'd seen such extravagance was in the house where she'd served as a slave those four awful years. Her stomach knotted. She'd learned early on that when a night held music and laughter and perfume and glittering baubles, the next day would hold slaps and scolding and threats as the mistress passed the cost for her indulgence along to her servants.

Her feet faltered. Her cheekbone ached with the memory of a hard hand striking it.

Mercy Williams seized on her hesitation, wrapping long-fingered hands around her arm and tugging her back a step. "Think this through, Prudence. Perhaps we all buck against the rules now and then, but thee knows as well as I that they are there for a reason. We have chosen a higher standard. *Thee* has chosen it—chosen it willingly and knowingly. I cannot bear to see thee now turning thy back on it."

Prudence pulled against the tug and shot her friend an exasperated look. Mercy had been her first true friend among the Friends. She was a year older, but something about her sweet, nurturing nature had drawn Prudence directly to her side on her first time venturing to Meeting.

Mercy had married just a month ago. Her new husband was a physician just returned from medical school back East, training now under old Dr. Thomas. And since her marriage, Mercy seemed more set than ever upon practicing her mother-hen tendencies with anyone who would let her.

"Mercy Williams." The new last name still felt odd on Prudence's tongue. She extricated her arm. "Thee knows me. I am not rebelling, I promise thee."

Mercy's blue eyes widened, and she leaned forward to hiss, "Thee is going to the *theater!*"

When Prudence had confessed it to her friend earlier that day, it had been with the request for prayers, because she did not want to fall prey to any allure of the glitter and gilt. And moreover, she didn't want to foul anything up and put Jason Willard in danger.

"In the third act," he had said while he sat in their kitchen last night, eating a slice of the bread she had baked, slathered in the butter she'd churned the day before, and topped with the last of the strawberry jam, "a character will come on stage, greeted by the name of Fiddle. I am told thee must listen especially to his lines. When he is supposedly describing where he witnessed a crime, he is really delivering instructions for us on where to meet the showboat tonight. Mark each description, each direction, each turn he says he made."

Her pulse thudded. Even now, Jason would be preparing to steal across the river as soon as darkness fell. He would meet up with the two brothers hiding on the Virginia side and sneak them into Ohio. "Thee knows the old Jenson barn?" he had asked her, his eyes serious over the cup of coffee Anna had poured for him. "As soon as thee has received the directions, thee must meet us there. Tell me what this Fiddle said. I will guide the young men to the rendezvous then, and thee will return safely home to Anna Barton." He'd offered her guardian a tight smile. "The risk to thy daughter is minimal, my friend, I assure thee."

Anna's smile had been lighter, yet just as somber. "This is the Lord's work, Jason Willard. Let the risk be what it may, I will not stop her from taking it."

Mercy Williams, on the other hand, seemed set on doing just that. When Mercy reached for her again, Prudence seized her friend's hands before they could twine around her arm and gave them a squeeze. "Mercy. Please, listen to me. This is not a simple pleasure outing, nor a rebellion. Did I not ask thee to hold me in prayer while I am about this business? Would I have done so if I were set on defying our Lord?"

Mercy pressed her lips together and darted a glance down the street, where two middle-aged Friends were closing up their shop for the evening and looking their way. Watching. No doubt wondering what a newly married young woman and a maiden were doing out at this dusky hour in town by themselves.

Prudence stepped closer to her friend. "I cannot tell thee details. But I ask thee to trust me."

Mercy's eyes flashed. "Thee promises thee is about nothing dire? Nothing underhanded? Nothing ignoble?"

That depended upon whose viewpoint one was looking from, Prudence supposed. The law would certainly deem it underhanded. And *dire* was a fair word to describe the plight of escaping slaves, to be sure. But ignoble it most assuredly was not. She swallowed and forced a smile. "I am doing what God has instructed me to do. With the full knowledge and approval of Anna Barton. Let that be enough for thee, my friend, I beg thee."

Mercy sighed, but Prudence could see the capitulation in her gaze. "Thee will be seen." She nodded toward the two scowling businessmen who were hesitating overlong outside their locked door. No doubt telling themselves they were seeing to the safety of the flock lest these poor little lambs go astray. "Thee may well have to answer for this before the Friends."

"So be it." She would tell them the truth, or whatever version of it the Lord put into her mouth. And if they judged her…that was not up to her. She could do only the part God set before her.

Mercy shook her head and turned away. But then she spun directly back, her brows drawn together in a scowl. "I saw Jason Willard walking to thy house last night, when my husband and I were taking a stroll. I confess, when thee came to visit today, I thought it would be to tell me that he is paying thee court. Instead, thee asked me to pray for this."

Prudence made no response but to hold her friend's gaze.

Realization gleamed in Mercy's eyes. "I know what work he does beyond the fields. My husband has lent him aid twice already since he returned home, when the...the sparrows he rescues are injured in their flight." She leaned closer, pitching her voice to the barest of whispers. "Is this what thee is about, Prudence Barton? Some part of his work?"

Prudence glanced again toward the lights and music and laughter of the *Gilded Palace*. "No one else would help."

Mercy huffed and twined their fingers together again. "To their shame. And to thy credit, if thee is doing it for them and the Lord rather than for Jason Willard's attention. I will detain thee no longer. But I will hold thee in prayer without ceasing until I get word thee is safely home."

There were no words to express Prudence's gratitude for that, and she couldn't waste any more time on reassurances. She squeezed her friend's fingers one last time, and then she pulled free and walked on.

Were it not nearly summer and the days so long, perhaps she could have made her way to the line of theatergoers without being recognized. But then, were it not nearly summer, a showboat would not have pulled into their docks. They came only during the warm season, meandering their way down the Ohio, entertaining each city along the way.

She had considered a disguise, but Anna had insisted that the best disguise was to be exactly who she was—a humble farm girl, slipping away for a night's revelry. No one would think anything of it.

No one but the ever-scowling Friends still hovering outside their door, anyway. She shot them a smile that she hoped looked innocent and prayed they would think she was visiting Martha Adams when she turned down the street on which the elderly woman lived—the street that would also take her to the docks.

Had she more time, she would have taken another path, one less direct, to throw the Friends off her trail. But Mercy, well intentioned as she was, had cost her precious minutes. If she didn't hurry, the ticket booth would close its windows before she could purchase her entry, and then she'd be in a fine spot.

If thee is doing it for them and the Lord...

As she hurried toward the now-short line at the ticket window, Prudence's fingers twisted in the simple gray shawl Anna had draped over her shoulders. She *was* doing it for the Lord, and for the slaves who deserved to have their humanity restored to them. But while she was in her bed last night after Jason had left, dreaming...well, she would be lying if she said the thought had not entered her mind that she could well earn his regard too, through this. It wasn't why she had agreed to do it. And she meant to keep to this path regardless. But even so. If ever he *did* walk to their house to pay her court, and if this was the means of his deciding to come, she would not object.

Was that wrong of her? To hope for more than the opportunity to help?

She took her place at the end of the line, her coins ready to purchase a ticket. It wouldn't be a good one, to be sure. Not like those decked out in their finest would have bought. She'd likely be standing, probably unable to see much of anything. But that was all right. She didn't need to see, just to hear.

"Cutting it close," the man at the ticket window said with a chuckle for the couple in front of her. "You'd better hurry along, now. Show starts in two minutes."

Two minutes! Prudence stepped forward the moment the couple moved away, pressing her coins to the counter. "One, please."

The man barely looked at her as he passed her a small paper ticket. "Get on with you. Hurry, now."

"Thank...you." She'd almost said *thee*. That would have been bad. She wasn't sure if everyone else in the world knew of the Quaker's injunction against theater-going, but speaking like a Friend would surely draw attention that she didn't want to draw. Not here. Not tonight.

She hurried into the wake of the couple again, following them up the ramp, onto the boat, hoping that everyone in the crowd would assume she was their daughter and just look right through her.

And she prayed with every step she took that these theater people who currently held lives in their hands could be trusted with them.

CHAPTER EIGHT

Janice stared for a moment at the bulletin board at the convenience store. The flyers for the dinner theater she'd been prepared to tack up were still in her hand. No need to put one here, apparently. Heidi or one of the others had beaten her to it.

And so had Keith. Right there beside the flyer for Heidi's show was the trifold brochure for the *Gilded Palace II*.

Still not sure what to think about him, she hurried back to her car. She had errands to complete on this Tuesday morning before returning to the inn to tackle her chores and the unfinished sewing.

Her next stop was the bank. She made her deposit and noted the showboat brochure tacked beside the murder mystery flyer on their bulletin board too. She frowned when she saw another brochure obscuring the flyer at her third stop of the day. It seemed a little odd that they were always together like that. And was it just an accident that it had covered up Heidi's flyer on that last one, or something more purposeful?

She still hadn't taken the time to talk to Heidi about Keith, but she really should. What if he was deliberately trying to compete with her? Show the fine citizens of Marietta that if they wanted a good show, his would outdeliver? She'd grant that his brochures sure looked more professional than Heidi's flyers. But then, he'd apparently already been in business for two seasons, spending the summers in other towns along the Ohio River. He had actual photographs of his shows to include. Heidi was still trying to get her business off the ground. Janice hoped Keith wasn't really trying to undermine Heidi, that they were better friends than that, but she would at least mention to Heidi that his brochures were everywhere her flyers were. If he *was* trying to compete, Heidi should at least be aware of it so she could step up her game.

Janice's last stop of the morning was the library. She returned the book she'd checked out two weeks before, along with a couple that LuAnn and Tess had sent along with her when she said she'd swing by there on her way home. She took a moment to browse their New and Featured shelf to see if anything caught her eye, grabbed a murder mystery by one of her favorite authors—she was in the mood, after all this prep work for the show—and headed to the check-out counter with her key-fob library card at the ready.

Then she froze. Absolutely froze as she faced the massive community bulletin board affixed to the wall. Here too! The *Gilded Palace II*, right beside Marietta Murder Mystery Dinner Theater! This definitely wasn't a coincidence.

Janice shook her head and readied her smile as she stepped up to the counter and the young, pretty librarian. "Morning, Maya."

"Good morning, Janice." Maya wielded her barcode reader on the fob, then on the book. "I hear there's going to be quite a show at the inn this weekend. Have you seen it yet? Is it any good?"

That just smoothed the rough edges right off Janice's mood, and her smile relaxed. "I have, and it's going to be so much fun. You should get your tickets before they sell out." How was that for optimism?

Maya nodded. "Yep, that's my plan. Figured I'd hop online during my lunch break and book them. When Heidi came in with her flyers, she mentioned that you guys set up her online ordering system for her. That was nice of you."

Janice laughed while Maya printed out her receipt and slid it between the pages of the book. "It wasn't me, I assure you. We let Tess handle all that stuff. I've never set up a website in my life."

Maya grinned. "Honestly, neither have I. But I certainly appreciate when others have done it well." She handed over the book. "Enjoy, and I'll plan on seeing you guys this weekend."

Janice smiled her way back out to her car. If everyone who said they were going to buy tickets really did, Heidi's venture would be a success yet. As she climbed back into her car and started it up, she said a prayer to that effect.

It took only a few minutes to reach the inn. After depositing her new book on her nightstand and scratching Tom's and Huck's heads in greeting, she got to work at her sewing machine.

Fabric and thread kept her company until it was time to head downstairs to help with the lunch rush at the café, and it wasn't until two o'clock that Janice really had the chance to find her friends and tell them what she'd found around town. She sank to a seat in one of the chairs in the office while she listed all the places with showboat brochures right beside or even partially obscuring the dinner theater flyers. "I mean, I understand he has to advertise too. It was just odd that they were always together, you know?"

"Yeah, I would have thought that strange too." LuAnn scooted her chair close to the desk and Tess's computer. "Have you learned anything interesting about this guy or his boat?"

Tess pulled up a browser she'd minimized. "Some. From what I could find, he bought an old sternwheeler about four years ago and began renovations to turn it into a showboat. This will be its third year in operation. A lot of what I could find were reviews on their previous two seasons. It seems to be doing pretty well, if you just go by that. Lots of four and five stars. All the complaints are isolated incidents or not the fault of the boat—like someone tall sitting in front of the reviewer, that sort of thing."

Janice reached for her cup of iced coffee. "So no other complaints about the owner being oddly interested in ripped-up plays?"

Tess chuckled. "Not on Yelp, anyway."

"What about the boat?" LuAnn tapped a finger against the desk.

Tess pulled up a page on her computer. "The sternwheeler they bought was previously used for river cruises along the Mississippi. It used to be called the *Mississippi Princess*."

"So what about the one they named it after?" Brows arched, LuAnn's history-loving smile emerged. "That *II* on the end of the name has to be of some significance, right?"

"It hadn't occurred to me to look that up. Let me see what I can find."

While Tess did another search and clicked on a few links, Janice swirled her straw through the creamy brown of her coffee. "I still need to talk to Heidi, just to get her take on all this. I should have before now, but she's been so stressed as it is..."

LuAnn nodded. "Not that there's anything wrong with competition, but awareness of it matters. We were certainly glad to know that Clint had B&B plans for his property. Definitely make sure she knows, even if she doesn't think it's a big deal."

Heidi would be coming over after school let out to prep a few more props before the actors were due to arrive at six. Janice would try to get her alone to talk to her before anyone else got there.

"Okay." Tess's eyes moved back and forth quickly as she read whatever article she'd brought up on her computer. "Looks like the original *Gilded Palace* was a showboat in the 1850s. Owned by someone named Michael Sullivan from Pittsburgh. It went down the Ohio River one summer, the Mississippi, then the Missouri, and then stuck with the Mississippi for several years before being used for troop transport during the Civil War. Looks like it was scrapped afterward."

"Was it an especially popular one or something?" Janice leaned in to peer at the screen herself. "Why name a new boat after it?"

"I have no idea. This says it enjoyed moderate success." Tess pointed at a paragraph. "Doesn't sound like it was particularly groundbreaking."

"Well, according to this brochure, Keith Johnson is from Pittsburgh. Maybe it's as simple as that. He chose a showboat from his hometown to name his own boat after." LuAnn had one of his brochures in hand and was reading the back flap.

Janice took another sip of her coffee. She could only shrug at that possibility, though it sounded reasonable enough.

LuAnn sighed. "Have you checked the ticket sales?"

"Not since the weekend." Tess winced. "Frankly, I haven't had the heart. I figure I'll check them while they're here tonight and give them an all-but-final count."

Echoing LuAnn's sigh, Janice pushed up from her chair, drink in hand. "Well, I'll talk to her when she gets here. In the meantime, I have a few things to finish up."

And plenty of praying to do while she worked.

"He and Kyle went to college together," Heidi said, in answer to Janice's question about how she knew Keith. They were outside, rigging up yet another fog machine. Thorn, their favorite handyman, had built a special platform for it on the patio. Heidi scooted the machine into a position that looked slightly precarious to Janice's eye, though she breathed a bit easier when Heidi secured it with some sturdy-looking wires. They were doing a full dress rehearsal tonight, and that included special effects.

Janice held the machine steady while Heidi twisted the wires. "So how are you going to manage all these special effects when it's a traveling show, and you can't set up more than a few hours ahead of time?"

Heidi chuckled. "Yeah, that's what Kyle wanted to know. We'll have to perfect a quick setup, and we'll at least scout the location first and take some photos so we know where to place things. But it's been really nice to have more leeway this first time. I appreciate you guys."

"You know we're happy to help."

"There. All secure."

Janice held the ladder steady while Heidi climbed back down. "So, back to Keith. He's more your husband's friend than yours?"

"Well, I've gotten to know him pretty well over the years too. We've seen a fair amount of him since we moved here, given his family connections to Marietta. Though not as much after he got married. I don't know his wife, but apparently she's firmly rooted in Boston."

Janice furrowed her brow. "Wait. Family connections here? His brochure says he's from Pittsburgh."

Heidi looked at her with an amused smile. "It does? I guess since I know the connection, it didn't occur to me you wouldn't make it too—though I guess the last name is so common, why would you? Keith *Johnson*. He's Leila's uncle."

Janice's smile, which had emerged to match Heidi's, froze. "Really? No, I didn't realize."

Her mind whirled. The missing foot pedal, all the brochures obscuring the flyers...was Leila behind it all, trying to help out her uncle at the cost of Heidi's enterprise? But why would she do that? Why, for that matter, wasn't she working for *him*? Why sign up for a little amateur theater that wasn't even off the ground yet?

"He's been so helpful." Heidi gathered up the extra length of cord and tucked it behind a few potted plants. "Given me tons of advice on how to get this thing going. I don't know how I could have done it without him."

Janice shook off her doubts and refreshed her smile. "That's nice of him. Especially since you're competition."

"Hardly!" Heidi laughed. "He's only in Marietta for a few weeks every other year. His big moneymakers are farther south. Really, Marietta is only a stop on his tour at all because his brother's here—I'm pretty sure he scheduled this year's dates to coincide with Leila's graduation. I bet he'd be willing to offer some deals for your guests. Special rates or something. You guys should chat about some promotions."

Assuming they could figure everything out, that would definitely be good for both businesses. "That's a thought. We'll talk to him about it. I also wanted to mention…" She hesitated, not even sure how to explain the questions his eagerness about the script had raised. "He offered to buy that partial script, sight-unseen. It struck us as a little odd. Like maybe he knew something about it we didn't…"

Heidi laughed again. "Oh, gracious, that's just Keith. He's obsessed about anything like that. You ought to see his collection on his boat. Seriously, he's bought some of the strangest things—what other people would call garbage—and found a way to make it interesting. Did you show it to him? See if he knew anything about it?"

Janice sighed. "Not yet. First we couldn't find a good time for it, and then his eagerness put us off a bit."

"He wouldn't try to cheat you, I can tell you that." Heidi grinned up at her. "A couple of years ago he bought a few old books from my aunt for maybe five bucks—he managed to sell one to a collector for a couple hundred a few months later and actually made a special trip here to split the profit with her."

That made Janice's unease lessen, to be sure. "That's good to know."

"All right." A note of happy finality in her voice, Heidi dusted off her hands and straightened. "I think we're set."

Janice nudged an extension cord out of sight with her toe. "It's kind of strange to realize that this time next week, it'll all be over."

"I know. I just hope some other bookings come in. I think I might have talked the manager of the bank into using us for a Christmas party, but that's quite a ways away. I'm hoping we can get some jobs over the summer."

"We've been praying that work will come your way."

Heidi's smile was vague. She never turned down Janice's prayers, but she never requested them either. Every time Janice mentioned anything having to do with faith or church over the years, her friend just changed the subject. Not that her ambivalence ever convinced Janice to do anything but pray harder.

Checking her watch, Heidi declared, "The girls should be here any minute. Are you sure you don't mind us using your space upstairs as our dressing room?"

"Not at all." Janice led the way back into the kitchen, where the scents from the day's lunch lingered, tantalizing and familiar.

"Did you eat yet? There's plenty of soup if you need a bite before you get started."

Heidi shook her head and pressed a hand to her stomach. "I'm too nervous to eat a thing. Isn't that weird? It's just dress rehearsal. And it's not like I've never directed a show before."

"This is different though. This is *yours*. Not the school's, not a community theater's. Yours."

"Yeah." Heidi blew a breath out. Even after a full day of school, her lips were still stained berry pink. Or maybe she'd reapplied her lipstick before coming over—Heidi was meticulous about such things. "If this fails, Kyle's going to be so mad. I've put a big chunk of our savings into it. All the equipment, the props and costuming...I mean, he said I could. And then he joked about how if it flops, we'll just retire to his hunting cabin in the mountains with no electricity instead of one of those nice communities where everyone has their own golf cart."

Janice could never quite decide if she liked Kyle Ingram or not. She'd only met him a few times over the years, but Heidi's stories didn't always settle well. Of course, Lawrence hadn't been perfect either—she'd had her own fair share of frustrations over the years and the occasional story to tell her friends about her husband's antiquated ideas about some things. Maybe his expectations chafed now and then, but they'd had a solid marriage, full of love and laughter and growing together. Heidi and Kyle seemed to have the same.

She sucked in a long breath of spicy air and exited the kitchen into the café.

Pretty soon Leila and Dempsey both arrived, and Heidi went upstairs with them to start getting ready. Janice held back, watching the trio disappear beyond the first landing. Leila seemed happy enough to be a part of the production. But she never seemed as fully engaged as the others. Even now, she'd come in with her phone in hand, her thumbs swiping.

"Goodness gracious goat, Janice," she muttered to herself. "You're being ridiculous. Heidi trusts her, so stop worrying."

Thankfully, LuAnn bustled in through the front door just then, saving her from either further suspicions or the subsequent self-chastising. LuAnn's arms were full of freshly cut flowers in purples and whites, setting loose a heady fragrance. "Hey there. Want to help me get these into vases? Then we can get our costumes on and maybe run through our song once before we get started."

Janice couldn't help but smile at the lilacs. They were some of her favorites. "Sure thing. I'll go get the vases."

With both of them working, it only took a few minutes to get the lilacs arranged in an assortment of tall vases. Janice took one into the sitting room and situated another on top of the mantel. A third took its place on an end table. When she came back out, LuAnn had adorned the front desk and the café.

Janice paused in front of them, closed her eyes, and breathed in the sweet scent. One of her favorite things about spring had always been the lilacs. She'd been giddy when she'd seen the buds on the bushes outside a week ago and realized they'd have armloads of blooms soon.

"Tess?" she heard LuAnn ask. "You ready to head up and change? I thought we could run through our song real quick before the guys get here."

Janice opened her eyes in time to see Tess move into the office doorway. Huck's nails clicked on the floor behind her, his tail wagging with enthusiasm.

LuAnn laughed and leaned down to scoop up the pup. "Have you been shadowing Tess today, Huckleberry?"

"We should probably try to keep him and Tom in your room this evening, LuAnn," Tess said. "I have a feeling the fourth-floor door will be opening a few too many times for Tom to resist the temptation of escape."

"Hopefully he hasn't escaped already." Janice kept an eye out as they headed upstairs—though that cat was an expert at hiding from them when he wanted to, which was any time he got out. Luring him back up, however, was usually just a matter of popping the top of a can of cat food, and he came charging in like he was half-starved.

The door was firmly shut at the top of the stairs though, and Tom was awaiting them in a patch of sunlight in the kitchen. While LuAnn herded the critters toward her room, Janice headed for her sewing room and fetched the costumes for the three of them.

Heidi, Dempsey, and Leila all sat around the table that had so recently held a dinosaur excavation, enough makeup spread out before them to make a girl's heart go pitter-patter, if she were inclined toward such things. Janice had never been obsessed, but she could admire a fine selection of cosmetics when she saw one. "Wow. You three come prepared."

As they laughed their agreement, she snatched the Inn Crowd's costumes from her rack. Since none of the actresses had changed yet—probably to avoid the risk of dropping makeup onto their dresses—she opted to leave them her bathroom and use either Tess's or LuAnn's.

Tess took her dress with lifted brows. "Did you talk to her about Keith?" she asked in a whisper.

Janice nodded. And shrugged. "She assured me he's a good friend, and she doesn't consider them in competition. And apparently he has gone out of his way not to even inadvertently cheat people when he buys old stuff from them. I think we can trust him, despite his attempt to sneak a look at the script. I still don't know why he did that, but..." Janice looked over her shoulder, though laughter was ringing out of her room. "Leila is his niece, apparently."

The arch of Tess's brows said she hadn't made the dubious Johnson connection either, but she made no comment. Just shook her head a bit and motioned toward her suite across the hall. "You can use my bathroom, if you want."

"Thanks." She continued down the hall first to hang LuAnn's sparkling gown on her door, then backtracked to Tess's suite.

Their dresses had begun their lives elsewhere—she'd found them at Antoinette's Closet and done some altering to give them a twenties flare.

Janice's was a blue to match her eyes. It had begun life as a simple sheath, but she'd added layer upon layer of fringe that would sway when she walked. She slid it on in Tess's bathroom and then smiled at her reflection. Lawrence would have loved it. His eyes would have sparkled when he caught sight of her, and that smile she loved would have taken over his lips.

Tears stung her eyes at the would-be memory, but she blinked them away and drew in a deep breath to fortify herself. Then she slipped out, padded down the hallway, and took up residence in their shared living room until her friends emerged.

LuAnn came out first, striking a pose in the entryway that made Janice laugh. "Perfect!" They'd found a white, shimmering dress for LuAnn that had at first been shapeless, but which Janice had turned into a drop-waisted beauty. "Get a load of you!"

LuAnn grinned. "I feel like one of those moody lounge singers we see in the movies." As if to prove her point, she wrapped a white feather boa around her neck and held a long cigarette holder—minus the cigarette at the end—to her lips. "You look like the elephant's instep yourself, Janice. A pretty dame if ever I saw one. Just check out your gams in that dress."

"What?" Janice laughed again, glancing self-consciously at her legs. "Did you use up all your twenties slang yet?"

"Not quite. I have a few more." LuAnn giggled too. "I'm saving them for Tess. And there she is! The bee's knees in those glad rags! The berries! A regular bearcat!"

Tess, decked out in a black and gold number that had required very little of Janice's attention, laughed as she came up alongside LuAnn, giving her a friendly swat with the decorative fan she held. "Ready to warm up our pipes, ladies?"

"You bet. I have the critters secured in my room." LuAnn pivoted to face the stairs.

Janice hummed a note, and the three of them began singing "My Melancholy Baby" in three-part harmony as they went down the stairs. She loved the piano and would enjoy accompanying their song, but there was something about a cappella harmony. It filled her with a beautiful resonance, echoing through each nerve, it seemed. And their stairwell always provided great acoustics. Too bad they couldn't just give their performance here.

They were halfway through the song by the time they actually reached the piano. Janice slid onto the bench, once again impressed with how talented her two friends were. They really ought to start having a few musical showcases on slow weekends. Maybe just with friends from church.

She'd run it by Pastor Ben and Paige and see what they thought. With their sweet baby Maxwell taking up their time, they might not be able to come themselves, but there were plenty of others at Christ Fellowship who might look forward to an evening out now and then.

After they'd gone through the song twice, LuAnn grinned. "Let's go over that other one too. Just for fun."

Janice laughed and pulled out the other sheet music they'd been debating on. "I'm game. Ready?"

None of them had memorized this one, so Tess and LuAnn both took a side and stood over Janice to read the words. Janice's fingers fumbled a few of the notes here and there but not too badly.

They'd all just sucked in a breath to belt out the first notes when a crash and a scream shattered the harmony.

CHAPTER NINE

By the time they'd rushed out to the patio, where the ruckus had originated, Janice was beginning to think from all the high-pitched squealing coming through the kitchen door that the sky had fallen.

But no. Only the fog machine. It slumped on the patio, in far too many pieces, while Heidi blubbered over it.

Dempsey had a protective arm around Leila. "You okay, Lei? You're sure?"

Leila nodded, mute.

"Man! Good thing you saw it coming, Dem, and pushed her out of the way." The men had obviously arrived while the Inn Crowd ladies were singing, given that it was Scott who spoke. His words shook with the fright.

Dempsey didn't seem to have heard him. She was urging Leila toward a chair. "Sit down, sweetie. Heidi, you too, before you ruin your makeup. Come on now." She gripped her director by the shoulders and eased her away from the fog machine's corpse. "It's not that big a deal. It's just a fog machine."

Heidi went where Dempsey urged, but her eyes were wide and glassy and remained fixed on the broken pieces. "I've had that machine for ten years. I bought it to use at the school when they said the budget didn't allow for one. I bought it myself."

"You can have mine," Dempsey said. "I bought one for that video I did, and it's almost exactly the same. You can have it, I won't need it again." Her smile warm, she nudged Heidi into another chair.

Heidi sucked in a breath. "I can't take your equipment, Dempsey—"

"You're not *taking* it." Dempsey gave her a warm smile and squeezed her hand. "I'm giving it, and that's that."

Heidi's lips wobbled. "That's so sweet of you. I can't thank you enough."

"You don't need to thank me. I just want to help."

"My hero." Heidi's attempt at a lighter tone ended in a quavering exhale. Her eyes fixed on the crumpled device. "How could it have just fallen like that? We had it secured. It was tied in place."

Rand, decked out in his mobster attire, squinted up at the little wooden platform. "Doesn't look like the platform came down."

It wasn't the platform alone that had been holding it in place though. There were also the wires.

Wires that now dangled down. "It must have been too heavy for the wires." Janice had noticed when Heidi put it up that the machine's position on the platform didn't look right—why hadn't she said something?

Heidi nodded. "Must have been. I should have let someone taller get the machine onto the platform, or taken the time to get a higher step stool. It was my own fault. I'm so sorry, guys. You sure you're okay, Leila?"

Leila nodded. And she did look fine. No pale cheeks, no shaking hands. She even offered a smile. "I'm okay. Just wishing I'd caught it on camera. We could've had a bloopers reel."

They all chuckled, but Janice's stomach still did a little flop. She appreciated Leila's comic relief, but even so, she could have been seriously injured.

Unless she'd known it was going to fall. Janice pressed her arms a little tighter against her middle and tried to banish the thought. While Rand gathered the broken pieces, she edged closer to the now-empty platform above the debris field and glanced up.

The wires dangled about six inches above her head. And though she didn't really know what they'd look like if they'd just snapped from the weight, all the crime shows and murder mysteries she'd consumed over the years said that surely they'd be frayed. Uneven. Show stress somehow or another.

Most of these, however, had neat edges, as if they'd been cut.

Rather than share this observation, Janice moved a step away again and buttoned her lips. She could be wrong. She'd ask Thorn to come and take a look at it tomorrow. But if she was right...that meant someone here had snipped them. Deliberate sabotage.

She glanced down while the talk continued to buzz around her, her eyes traveling across the flagstones, the blades of grass trying to grow between them, the shimmer of sunlight on a trail of stray gold glitter, the tiny purple flowers dotting the grass. Why would anyone do this? To try to cause problems for the theater group? Or for some more sinister reason?

To her mind, it would have been a hard thing to time, so trying to injure someone in particular didn't make a whole lot of sense. Sabotage seemed much more likely.

Her gaze drifted to Leila for a moment and then skittered away. How many times could sabotage happen around a particular person before it stopped being a coincidence?

"What's up?" LuAnn asked the question in a whisper when Janice stepped back over to her and Tess.

"I don't know," Janice murmured, too aware of all the people nearby to want to say more. "Later."

Tess lifted a brow, clearly knowing Janice had noticed something, but she just nodded.

"There we go." Rand stood, the pieces in his arms, and offered a tight smile. "I'll see if I can do anything with it. I have my doubts, but if I can… I'll just run it to my truck, okay?"

Janice tapped a finger against her arm. Rand had cause to be upset with Heidi too. She'd threatened to fire him, after all. Maybe he'd wanted to take a bit of revenge, cause a little setback. He certainly knew enough about wiring to pull it off, and he had the tools right there in his truck. And no doubt he'd been the last one to arrive, as usual. With the help of a chair for a stepladder, he could have made a few quick snips on his way inside from the parking lot.

Not that she wanted to accuse Rand. Or anyone.

Heidi stood. "Okay. Enough boo-hooing. Everybody ready?"

Rand was tromping back from the parking lot even then. "I am. We start inside, right?"

A flicker of irritation sparked in Heidi's eyes but quickly banked. "Yes." The *s* hissed, an unspoken but clear message: *How many times do we have to go over this?* Or maybe *If you'd ever shown up for the start of a rehearsal, you'd know that.*

Rand unfortunately had to stay on Janice's list of people who might have a bone to pick with Heidi.

They all filed back inside, heading for the front entryway. Heidi was pointing to the parlor, motioning with her hands. "So we'll have all the costumes for the guests set up in here, and the inn's mantel is the perfect backdrop for the photos. Leila, is your mom still willing to do those?"

Leila nodded and lifted her phone. "Go pose for me, Dem."

Dempsey never needed to be asked twice to pose for a photo, it seemed. She practically skipped over to the mantel and bent over a bit in front of it, hands on her knees in the classic twenties pose as if she were about to break into the Charleston at any moment.

Janice, standing behind Leila as she was, watched as she touched the button to take a photo and with a few swipes applied a black-and-white filter.

"My sister will be in charge of handing out the costumes." Heidi directed this to Janice. "I think you worked with her on our production of *The Wizard of Oz*, didn't you?"

Janice nodded. It was one of the last school productions she'd been a part of before she retired. Heidi's sister, Sophie, had volunteered her time, and she and Janice had spent many an hour together painting the Tin Man's costume and trying to sew straw into the ends of the Scarecrow's sleeves. Fake straw, that is, because the actor had broken out in a rash when they'd tried to go authentic. "Sophie and I are pals. I know she'll take great care of them."

Heidi nodded and even tried to smile. "So as each guest or couple gets in character, Leila's mom, Marisol, will get a picture of them. With their permission, we'll be posting them all online, tagging them, and thereby spreading the word some more. Idea courtesy of Leila, of course."

Leila saluted.

Heidi continued, the tension releasing from her voice with each word. "Scott, you're in charge of the photocopies of the worksheets still, right?"

Scott grinned. "My employee discount to the rescue. I'll do them tomorrow."

"Great. Luke—"

"My aunt's catering service is ready to go. She called me last night and talked my ear off for an hour about how she and Miss Winnie have had a grand ol' time figuring it all out, and she can't *wait* to come and cook on Big Red." Luke put on a full country drawl, presumably in imitation of his aunt, snapping his fingers in emphasis.

Heidi actually chuckled now. "We need to get her the final numbers for prep. Tess, have you checked the sales lately?"

Beside her, Tess shifted. "No, not yet. Want me to do that now?"

"Would you please?" Heidi turned to LuAnn while Tess scurried away. "We'll make it clear where in the inn the guests can go and where they can't, but Scott is printing up a few signs to direct them to the right places too, like we discussed."

LuAnn smiled. "Perfect."

"Okay." Sucking in a deep breath and letting it out with a whoosh, Heidi clapped her hands together. "Let's get this dress rehearsal started. Rand, you got the sound equipment set up earlier, right?"

Janice looked at him with lifted brows. She hadn't seen him around the inn doing it, but LuAnn was nodding, and so was Rand. He must have stopped over while she was out. And had apparently disguised the speakers enough that she hadn't even noticed them. Excellent.

He held out his hand. "I'll go put the CD in, if you want."

Heidi nodded and moved toward a bag stashed behind a chair.

"Holy cannoli!"

Tess's shriek brought them all around. Dreading what might have gone wrong now, Janice took off at a run, along with LuAnn, toward the office, beating everyone else there by a few steps.

Tess had turned her chair toward the door. Her mouth had fallen open, her eyes were wide, and she was motioning toward the screen. "We've—you've—Heidi—you've sold out! Except I hadn't put a number on it—it didn't seem relevant—so we've oversold! By fifteen tickets."

Oversold? Janice blinked at her friend for a moment, but Tess's expression didn't change. She still looked dumb-founded. A combination of thrilled and panicked. Why hadn't she put a limit on the number of tickets sold on the website? Though really, it hadn't seemed to be an issue. They'd sold so few...

Heidi stumbled forward. "What? How did—wow." She spun to face her crew, and a slow smile brightened her face. "Whatever you guys have been doing, it must have worked!"

So maybe all those showboat brochures tacked up over the flyers hadn't caused any harm. That was good to know. Though still, Janice shook her head. "What are we going to do? We can't fit that many people in here."

Everyone fell silent. After a moment, Heidi said, "Maybe we can do a second show the following weekend. I'll take tomorrow off and call the last people who bought tickets—they did have to provide a phone number, right, Tess?"

Tess nodded. "Phone number, email address, and name. And if necessary, we can refund the ones who bought after what should have been the cutoff."

"It'll be better if we can get them to agree to a show the next weekend." Heidi squeezed her eyes shut. "I can find a place somewhere, I'm sure. I'll call around. I mean, it'll put us into Memorial Day Weekend, but surely there's something available. Or we could do a weekday."

Janice exchanged a glance with her friends, who both gave her a discreet nod. "Let us check on next Saturday. We're completely full, but half the guests are attending some sort of reunion together and won't be back Saturday night until ten anyway—they asked what time we lock the doors. We can call the others and make sure they don't have any problems with it.

The big problem would be the clues you're planting in the rooms. Fine when it's your family, but..."

"We can rework that—have the clues in the hallway or something. And you could offer the guests discount tickets." Heidi bounced a bit on her toes and beamed at Tess. "If we can divide them up, then there would still be room on a second night for that, right?"

Tess nodded. "We could fit fifteen more. We'll likely lose a few though. I'm so sorry. I should have filled in that max-available field, but I didn't when I set it up because we were still talking about it, and then...well..."

"It's okay. It'll be good even." Heidi let loose a laugh and grabbed the shoulder closest to her—Scott's—and gave it an excited shake. "We've sold out!"

Rand poked his head in. "That's great. But, um...the sound equipment isn't cooperating. It was working fine earlier, but..."

Dempsey rolled her eyes and nudged Rand aside with a hand. "Move aside, Daddy-o. Let the young'uns handle the music."

Rand chuckled and stepped back with a grand sweep of his arm. "By all means. Assuming you know what a CD is. It's one of those circle thingies that has a hole in the center—the things music used to be on before you just downloaded it all. Kinda shiny..."

"Dinosaur technology," Luke finished with a grin. He and Dempsey moved in the direction of Rand's gesture. "Don't worry, we know how to use all forms of dino tech. CDs, eight-tracks, wax cylinders..."

Rand pulled Luke's hat down over his eyes as he walked past.

Janice turned back to look at Tess's screen, still half expecting a refresh to drop those numbers back down to six. How in the world had they sold so many over the weekend? "I don't suppose you had a 'how did you hear about us' field on the purchase page?"

Tess shook her head. "We can ask when they come in on Saturday."

"And we should," Heidi agreed. "So we know what was working. Aw, man, I hope this means people will be booking us for more shows."

"I bet it was that radio spot you did on Sunday." Rand leaned into the doorway, grinning at Heidi. "You made it sound like the most fun to be had in decades."

Janice hadn't heard it—it had run while she was at church. But she smiled. "Whatever it was, it worked."

A minute later, music burst into the inn, bright and fun. Heidi clapped and shooed everyone out of the office. "Young'uns to the rescue. Thanks, guys!"

Dempsey sashayed back over with a grin, Luke with a comical scowl as he brushed off his sleeve. "Wow, Dem. Can't you cut out some of the sparkly stuff? I'm going to start calling you Tinkerbell."

"Just think of the fun special effects we could pull off if she could really make you fly with a sprinkle of pixie dust." Heidi winked at him and then said in her director-voice, "Places, everyone! Let's get this show on the road!"

"Are you sure? I was hoping I was wrong."

Thorn shook his head and flicked the end of the cords that had been holding up the fog machine. "Three of the four anyway. The last one broke. See?" He held the four together, bending down a bit to show her what he meant.

She compared the four. Honestly, they didn't look *that* different to her. But she supposed, maybe, she could see a bit of a difference between the neat snips of the first three compared to the stretched-out look of the fourth. She nodded.

Thorn motioned to the all-but-new fog machine Dempsey had dropped off that morning. "Think you can hand that up to me?"

Janice hefted it and raised it up for him. "We shouldn't leave it up until Saturday, should we? I think it's supposed to rain tomorrow."

"We won't. Just want to make sure I have a better rig set up and ready to go. Then all we have to do on Saturday is tie it in." He slid it onto the platform—more securely than Heidi had done, and at a more reasonable angle in Janice's opinion. "Bev sure is looking forward to the show."

Janice grinned. "You guys bought tickets?"

"She and Laura decided it sounded like fun." Thorn snorted a laugh. "All the times I've mentioned it didn't faze them at all, but they see a picture or something on Facetagram, and it's the only thing they can talk about."

Janice chuckled at his mashing of the social networks. "So Laura and Jake are coming too?"

"Yep." Thorn fished a zip tie out of his pocket and used it to secure something on the platform.

"This weekend or next? Did Tess call them yet about the need for a second date?"

Her old friend glanced down at her with a question on his face. "Don't know. I've been here all day. You guys overbook or something?"

Janice nodded. "We didn't expect that to be possible—Tess forgot to fill in the maximum number of tickets field on the website."

Thorn grinned and shook his head. "I don't imagine we care much which weekend we go. In fact, next weekend might be better. Laura mentioned that her favorite babysitter was out of town until the day *after* the show."

"Let's hope many others say the same thing." Janice took a step back to survey his work. "That looks way more secure than when Heidi did it."

"I could have stopped by to put the first one up." Thorn climbed down from his stepladder to look up at it too. "If I had, it would have taken more than a couple of snips to bring it down, and I'd have been willing to call it part of the price of building the platform." He glanced down at his hands and grimaced. "Good grief, whose machine was this? It's covered in junk."

"Junk?"

He lifted his hands, showing them to be liberally coated in a fine gold glitter.

Janice laughed. She couldn't help it. One didn't look at Thorn, with his military haircut, his cross tattoo, and his work clothes, and think, *Guy who likes glitter.* "Paisley will love it."

Thorn grinned. The mere mention of one of his two grandchildren was enough to soften his gruff exterior. "With my luck, she'll start going around saying 'Princess Granddad.'"

That set Janice laughing again. "We can get you a crown. I bet Dempsey has a few to spare."

"You're hilarious." But he was still grinning as he slapped his palms against his jeans. Apparently he wanted them to be sparkly too. "All right, I'll get this thing down again. I'm happy to come over on Saturday to put it back into place before the show. Anything else I can do to help?"

"I don't think so, but rest assured we'll let you know if we think of something." She gave him a smile and headed inside to find LuAnn and Tess and give them an update.

Knowing them, they'd snatch a few minutes at some point today to make a suspect list.

Janice noticed the stack of worksheets for the play that Luke had dropped by an hour ago, sitting on the front desk. She already knew who all their real-life suspects were—and they were the same people whose stage names were on those pages.

Was it okay to be almost amused by that, since no one had gotten hurt and no serious damage was done? It was more a prank than serious sabotage, after all. Regardless, while the guests were trying to figure out who "killed" Luke's character on Saturday, Janice and her friends could be solving their own mystery. *The Case of the Crashing Fog Machine.* Who knew, maybe the same culprit had been responsible for hiding the pedal of her sewing machine. And messing with the sound equipment the other night. The college kids had fixed that easily enough, sure, but Rand had huffed in frustration when they'd said the wires had been switched around. The implication was that he'd just done it wrong.

But he hadn't. The system had worked fine when he tested it earlier, according to LuAnn. Someone had deliberately switched the wires afterward.

Silly things. Petty things. Meant to fluster them, perhaps? Janice couldn't be sure. But she would definitely be keeping an eye out for any more pranks.

Tess was just hanging up the phone in the office when Janice poked her head in.

"Hey," Tess said, marking something on a sheet of paper beside her. "Looks like this is going to work out rather well. The guests not attending the reunion were pretty enthusiastic about getting discounted tickets to the show. Well, the Mulligans already had plans, but they didn't mind that the inn would be used in their absence. They're the only ones with kids that weekend."

Janice went over to glance down at the list. "Are we calling any of the theater guests for Heidi? Need my help?"

"Yes, and sure. Here, you can take this group." Tess handed her a sheet of paper with a dozen names on it. "I'd already broken them up into batches. We're going to start with the later purchases and see if anyone wants to move dates, moving to the earlier one if necessary. Update it in the computerized system as things change." Tess waved a hand at her screen, which showed the admin page of the ticket sales site. It still had fifty sales showing for this Saturday, and eight for next week.

Janice raised her eyebrows. "Are those new sales for next week or have some already agreed?"

"They're the inn guests. And apparently two that Heidi must have rescheduled already. I've paused the sales until we get this sorted. We probably won't have room for many more next week."

Janice stared at the screen for another moment. "A far cry from the six it was at before, isn't it? Goodness gracious goat. Have you asked anyone you talked to already where they heard about it?"

"I've only talked to our own guests thus far, who hadn't." Tess smiled and pulled another sheet of names forward. "But you're welcome to ask the ones you call."

Janice chuckled. "I'll use the front desk phone." Taking her sheet of paper to the padded stool behind the front desk, Janice made herself comfortable. The event was going to be a smashing hit...as long as nothing else came crashing down.

CHAPTER TEN

Three days later, the inn was buzzing with life and laughter. Janice sat at the piano, her fingers teasing a ragtime song from the keys. The first of Heidi's two CDs—the one for before the show—had vanished. Or been misplaced. Given how scattered her friend seemed tonight, Janice wasn't willing to file that one under the "suspicious happenings" column when it was just as likely that Heidi had simply carried it around for half an hour and set it down somewhere.

But Janice had assured her that it was no cause to panic and had slid onto her piano bench quite happily. She'd gathered a selection of 1920s-era songs when she and the Inn Crowd were searching for which one they'd like to sing, including the book open on the baby grand's music rack now. She had more than enough material to provide the background music for the half hour before the show started.

She glanced over to the parlor side of the room, where a new group of guests had come in and were laughing as Sophie acquainted them with the costume rack and told them to pick their look. Every time Janice glanced over she saw that the men at least put on a hat and the ladies an accessory. Many went all out and chose dresses or, for the men, jackets and vests.

They'd each be given new identities for the night, names written in an art deco font on their name tags that matched the ones on the envelope each guest was handed. Inside were a few sentences of backstory for each and occasionally special instructions that they were to play out during the event. Some of them would find themselves part of the mystery—one was even the "killer"—but no one would know who until the clues had been laid out. At the end of the night, the fictional murderer would be given a special prize for playing along—one of Winnie's gorgeous cakes. Most of them looked quite eager to enter their life of crime and clutched their sealed envelope with exaggerated gusto.

Janice hummed along with the melody of the song, even easing into the words on the chorus. Reorganizing the event into the two weekends had ended up working just fine. Quite a few of the original ticket holders were actually glad to have the option, and others had no preference, so they were willing to change their reservations without a qualm. And within a few hours of opening sales again to fill the last few spots for next weekend, the show was sold out.

Heidi had ended up booking a night at the old theater too, for the first weekend in June, and *it* was nearly sold out. Thus far they had no idea how the "traveling" aspect of her vision would take off, but the "theater" side was certainly picking up steam.

Janice smiled into her sheet music and let the vocals taper off again. If those pranks had been meant as sabotage, they were failing. Spectacularly. And Janice couldn't be happier for her friend.

Someone rustled up behind her, and Janice recognized the sound of LuAnn's dress before she even glanced over her shoulder so her eyes could prove her ears correct. On the next chorus, LuAnn's alto paired with Janice's soprano. Tess was no doubt taking care of a few last-minute business-type details, after which she'd lock the office.

LuAnn kept singing into the next verse, so Janice continued as well. The live music added a nice touch, she thought. Maybe they would do it again next week. Though after that, when the theater moved away from the inn, Heidi would just have to keep track of her CDs.

Eventually Tess did join them, and soon the influx of guests seemed to taper off.

"I think everyone has checked in," Tess said in an undertone while Janice improvised on the keys so she could look at her friend instead of the music. Tess's gaze was on the other side of the room, where Sophie was straightening the few costumes remaining on the rack. Leila's mom, camera in hand, was waving to one last couple as they made their way to the café.

Janice nodded. "Heidi said she would give me the signal to stop playing once everyone is seated." After that, they'd have a short break while the opening drama unfolded, then their big vocal number that was part of the production. "I trust her caterer and servers showed up?"

"Yep, they were all in the kitchen and café setting out the appetizers before I came in here. Looks like all's set." LuAnn smoothed back a lock of hair and glanced at the door.

Tess gave her a friendly elbow and an impish grin. "Wishing Brad hadn't changed his reservation to next week?"

"Stop it." LuAnn rolled her eyes and faced the piano again. "I'm watching for Heidi."

As Tess laughed, Janice turned to the next page in her songbook. By the time she finished it, Heidi had indeed come in and given her the nod to stop, so she let the last note fade away. From the café and foyer she could hear laughter and chatter dying down as well.

Then came Heidi's voice over the speakers Rand had rigged. "Thank you so much for joining us tonight for the debut of the Marietta Murder Mystery Dinner Theater." She paused for the clapping and whistles. "Tonight we'll be presenting an original mystery called *Son of the Gun*. Have you all had a chance to look over the information you were given in your envelopes? Some of you are part of the show! You'll also notice that at each seat, there's a small clipboard with a sheet of paper. This is to help you keep track of the clues you gather. As the meals are served, the play will get underway. You'd better pay attention! Everyone who correctly solves the mystery will be entered to win one of those two delicious-looking cakes sitting in the back."

Even from here, Janice could hear the appreciative *oohs* and *ahhs* and shouts as the guests got a load of the cakes Heidi had hired Winnie to make—one for the winner and one for the murderer.

"Clues have been planted all over the inn, and you'll have to go and search for them—in the parlor, in here, on the second floor—only in the rooms with open doors, now—and even outside on the patio. After the first act, you'll be free to work off that delicious dinner and go on the hunt for clues. We'll make sure everyone is back for the second act and dessert, and then see if you've solved the mystery. Is everybody ready?"

A chorus of whistles and applause.

"Here we go!"

Background music from the CD took the place of Heidi's voice. Janice exchanged a grin with her friends and rubbed her hands together.

Tempting smells had been creeping through the inn for a while now, but they intensified as the play got underway and the dinner was served, making Janice's stomach growl. But they'd get their turn to eat while the guests were running around collecting clues.

Her eyes moved to a few of them. The framed photo of the actors, black and white and elegant, on the mantel. A handwritten letter half tucked under an old book on one of the end tables. The mantel clock, stopped with its hands reading two thirty-two.

The actors were all miked, so the audience could hear the story as it progressed without any problem. And as far as Janice could tell, no one so much as fumbled a word. The story unfolded exactly as it was supposed to, the background music providing the perfect mood for each moment.

"They've really done a fantastic job," LuAnn murmured, leaning against the piano.

"They have. I'm so glad the sales took off like they did." Tess fiddled with the long rope of pearls she wore. She took a seat beside Janice on the piano bench, facing out instead of toward the keyboard.

Janice slid the correct sheet music to the front of her music stand. They only had another couple of minutes until they were up. "Me too."

Soon their cue came through the speakers, and Tess stood again, moving to LuAnn's side. Janice glanced over at the doorway to see that Heidi had come in. Heidi gave her a nod, and Janice placed her fingers on the cool ivories. She launched into the intro, vaguely aware of more bodies crowding the room. She didn't turn to watch them though. She kept her gaze on the music.

They sang just as they had rehearsed it so many times, their voices blending in the way that Janice loved. She knew Tess and LuAnn were enjoying themselves every bit as much as she was, striking their poses on certain words much as she provided little flourishes here and there. By the time the song was finished and the audience clapping and cheering, Janice couldn't wipe the grin off her face. She slid off her bench to stand with the others and took a bow.

The crowd then began to mill about in search of clues as another CD of background music came on. If the laughter, whispers, and excited shrieks were any indication, the audience was having a grand time. Janice followed LuAnn out of the room, toward the kitchen, craning her neck to see a few groups dashing up the stairs to the guest rooms that were open tonight for the hunt—just two, rented by Heidi's family. They had all their belongings in a third room for now.

They wouldn't be able to have those rooms open next week, but it was totally worth it when one of the first guests to get up there shouted, "Oh! Look how gorgeous! This would be perfect for our girls' weekend, Mom!"

"Yes!" LuAnn danced in a circle as they entered the now-empty café. "We'll have to thank Heidi for the exposure."

Janice laughed her way into the kitchen. It was odd to see unfamiliar servers in here, but Winnie hadn't at all minded *not* coming in for an extra shift. Luke's aunt, Shelly, was humming along with the music and spooning chocolate sauce over the plates of decadent-looking chocolate something or another. Her wait staff was coming in with trays of dishes and going out again with cleaning cloths.

By the time the guests had finished up their clue hunting, dessert and coffee would no doubt be ready and waiting for them.

Shelly looked up at their entrance and gave them a big smile. "I'm going to steal your stove, ladies. Think it'll fit on the roof of my car?"

They laughed, and Janice looked at the massive, shining contraption lovingly dubbed Big Red. "Winnie would hunt you down in a heartbeat."

"I'll fight her off." She made a jabbing motion with her chocolate-covered spoon, an exaggeratedly fierce expression on her face. She was a jolly-looking woman, all round cheeks and fluffy hair and smiles. And not nearly so pronounced a drawl as Luke had given her in his imitation, though Janice did detect a bit of Appalachia.

"I put plates aside for you guys," one of the servers said—a pretty girl probably in her late teens. She motioned toward three beautifully arranged plates sitting on the end of the table, out of the way.

The first bite of Shelly's chicken had Janice closing her eyes in bliss. "Goodness gracious goat, Shelly. This is phenomenal. Leave a business card somewhere, will you? We love being able to recommend great options for people when they book events here."

Shelly grinned at them. "I slapped a magnetic one on your fridge when I came in—audacious of me, I know."

LuAnn laughed. "Forward thinking, that's all. Perfect."

Through the kitchen windows, open to the May breeze, they could hear people out on the patio, and a whiff of the fog machine's smoke teased Janice's nose too. She wrinkled it against the funny odor and breathed in her garlic mashed potatoes instead. Good to know it was working at least, she supposed. The interior one wouldn't be turned on until the second act got started.

After they finished their meal, they meandered back into the café just as the guests were doing the same from the foyer. The tables now had dessert plates before each chair, coffee cups at the ready, and water glasses refilled, which earned more exclamations of appreciation from the returning audience.

"Meow."

For a moment, Janice assumed someone was just making cat noises, though she couldn't imagine why. Then a brush of something soft around her ankles brought her gaze down to the floor, where Tom was winding around LuAnn's leg.

"What in the world are you doing down here?" Her face a mixture of outrage, fondness, and confusion, LuAnn bent down to pick up the cat. He nuzzled her chin, his purr loud enough to be heard over the growing chatter of the crowd.

Tess was frowning. "Good question. He was locked in your room, wasn't he, Lu? Even if someone went back upstairs for something after we came down, he shouldn't have gotten out."

Something tightened in Janice's chest. They'd all locked their bedroom doors—the only one left open had been her sewing room and bathroom, for the cast to use.

LuAnn and Tess must have been thinking the same thing. With a shared glance that needed no words, they all started for the café's exit and the stairs. A few stragglers passed them on the staircase—three women clutching their clipboards and smiling in their boas, drop-waist gowns, and cloche hats—but the trio didn't slow as they bypassed them on their way up.

The door to their apartments was closed. But obviously it hadn't been at some point. LuAnn reached it first and swung it open with her free arm. Tom seemed happy enough snuggled against her chest, no doubt getting fur all over her dress.

The single lamp they'd left on still shone from the living room, lighting enough of the kitchen and hall that anyone who needed to come up would be able to see where they were going, and the light was on in Janice's sewing room too—not a surprise, since that was the dressing room. She went to peek in, but it was empty.

Of course it was empty. While the guests had been collecting clues, the actors had still been in character, interacting with the audience. They wouldn't have been up here.

"Maybe a guest, ignoring the off-limits sign?" Tess pursed her lips and examined the closed doors. "Maybe you forgot to lock your door, LuAnn."

"I was sure I did." But when LuAnn put a hand on her knob, she turned it without any resistance, and Huck greeted her with a yip. At least he wasn't running free somewhere too. But then, he wasn't quite as sneaky about escaping as Tom was. "And even if I didn't, that doesn't explain how Tom got out. Clever as he is, he can't open doors."

Tess unlocked her door and slipped into her own room, switching on the light.

Figuring she'd better check hers too, Janice pulled out the key from the hidden pocket of her dress and unlocked her door. She flicked her light switch on and stood there for a moment, looking around. Nothing seemed out of place. The scarf she had considered wearing was still draped half on her bed, half off. The pair of shoes she'd decided against was tumbled against the closet door.

She slid into the hallway again, locking the door once more behind her, and rendezvoused with the others at LuAnn's end of the hall. "Anything amiss?"

LuAnn shook her head. "I don't know. Something didn't seem right, but it could just be paranoia. I did check my jewelry box, and nothing was missing. Laptop's still on my desk. If someone was snooping around, they don't seem to have taken anything obvious. Tess?"

Tess shook her head. "Nothing's disturbed in mine that I could tell, and it was still locked."

"Maybe I *did* just forget to lock my door. I guess one of the cast members could have opened it by mistake, thinking it was Janice's sewing room." LuAnn brushed a bit of cat fur from her torso and pasted on a smile that didn't convince Janice for a second. "Regardless, there's no point in hovering up here. To paraphrase Shakespeare, 'All the inn's a stage, and we are mere players.'"

Tess didn't even attempt a smile. "Let's get back down to our post and see if anyone looks as though they've been snooping around up here."

Act Two was in full swing by the time they reached the main floor. Janice didn't want to cause a distraction by slipping back into the café, so instead she turned toward the parlor. And froze when her eyes caught on the office door.

The *open* office door.

CHAPTER ELEVEN

Janice stepped into the office behind Tess, her gaze searching the room. Maybe LuAnn had forgotten to lock her bedroom, but they always locked the office. The fact that it was open now meant someone had gone beyond curiosity and into unlawful entry.

There was nothing obviously out of place, but Tess made a beeline for the computer, muttering, "The screen should have shut off. It hibernates after twenty minutes."

LuAnn headed for where the wall safe was hidden. It only took her a minute to have it open. Janice slid up behind her. She'd been the one to put the guests' jewelry in there—and there it still was. Two slim velvet cases, right beside the cash envelope.

"Here." LuAnn handed her the boxes. "Make sure they're not empty. I'll check the cash."

Janice took them, but it only required a couple of squeaking box hinges and about five seconds to show her that the diamond tennis bracelet was still in the one and the enormous amethyst pendant in the other. "Good here." She slid the boxes back in.

"Same." LuAnn returned the cash and closed the safe. "Tess?"

Janice pivoted and saw Tess sitting at her desk, clicking into different things on the computer. "It really shouldn't have been on, but it was still on the login screen where you enter the password. That's something, I guess. I don't think anyone actually saw anything on here. Not that there's anything interesting to see anyway."

LuAnn tilted her head. "Good. I mean, I can think of plenty of nefarious reasons someone might want access to reservations, but let's hope that's just my overactive imagination and not what someone was really trying to do."

"Yeah, let's. At least since they failed." Janice shuddered, then jumped a bit when a crash sounded from outside the office. A planned one, but still. She splayed a hand over her racing heart. "They must be about finished. That sounded like Dempsey's fit of rage."

"Yeah. Let's go back out. We'll check things again after everyone is gone." Tess shut down the computer.

Janice led the way out the door just in time to hear Heidi speaking again, inviting everyone to finish up their worksheets and decide on whodunit. They slipped back into the café, where the actors were all standing against the wall, smiling and looking pleased. A hum arose as the guests quietly compared notes, a few laughs trickling out.

Everyone looked as though they'd had a great time. No one looked particularly guilty. But someone obviously was.

Heidi flashed them a grin and then turned back to the crowd. "Okay, everybody finished? Let's see who's going to get to take home those awesome cakes—you'll notice they're now boxed up. One will go to a winner selected from those of you who got the answer right—and the other will go to our culprit. A condolence prize for being branded a criminal tonight. And sorry, Don, but that would be you—the character of Backhanded Ben-o. Did you guess correctly?"

The expected groans and cheers rang out, and the actors moved around the tables to jot down the names of everyone who had the right name written on their papers as the audience themselves explained to each other why Ben-o was the logical culprit. A few minutes later all the names went into Luke's fedora—he was probably glad to be up off the floor, finally—and he pulled out the winner, a woman named Marcy, whom Janice had met a few times over the years but didn't know well.

Heidi led the clapping for the winners. "Congratulations! I know you'll enjoy Winnie's creation. Now, did you all have fun?" More cheering. Heidi grinned. "I am so glad to hear it. We'll be doing new mysteries every month, and you can book us for your parties and events or just join us again next month at the theater. You'll find a brochure at your seat with our information—be sure to check our website and social media frequently to see what we're up to next! Everyone have a great night, and if you'd like to leave a video message for our website, Marisol will be doing those when you return your costumes. Thanks, all!"

Janice tucked herself out of the way with LuAnn and Tess as most of the crowd meandered toward the foyer. Heidi's family and a few of the other audience members were swarming her with congratulations and excitement, and she was beaming like a supernova. Janice had to smile to see it, even though with one eye she was watching all the guests. Most were simply going into the parlor to return their costume pieces to Sophie and film their short endorsement videos. But if anyone so much as glanced at the office door, she was ready to pounce.

"You're kidding." Heidi's horror looked genuine. "Who would do that?" She turned her wide eyes on her cast, though they all looked just as taken aback about the knowledge that someone had broken into the office and gone into LuAnn's rooms. "Anyone see anything?"

They all shook their heads, claiming, just as Janice had thought, that they were all here on the ground floor for the entire evening and had known not to let the animals out.

Janice slipped back into the office as they mused. Tess had unlocked it once everyone but the staff was gone—and it certainly hadn't been their goal to put a damper on the crew's victorious evening. But if someone had seen anyone going up the stairs to the third and fourth floors or coming into the office, they had to know.

She turned in a circle, not knowing what she expected to see now that they hadn't seen earlier. Everything was still neat and orderly. The computer was still shut down. The safe was secure.

Then, when she was facing the door again, her eyes caught on a slip of bright blue. Frowning, she moved toward it, and it fluttered up against the filing cabinet. It took her a moment to realize it was a feather. A blue feather that had to have come from one of the boas. She picked it up and twirled the bit of fluff in her fingers.

It could have come in with one of the three of them, maybe. Been stuck to a hem or a shoe. She eyed the space between the door and the bottom of the floor, but there wasn't clearance enough there for it to have blown underneath.

No. There were only two ways it could have gotten there. Either they brought it in when they noticed the door cracked open or the person who'd broken in had lost it.

The first option wasn't unlikely—but given that the second, if true, was the only lead they had, it seemed worth entertaining the possibility. Janice stalked back out with the scrap of feather held high. "I may have found a clue."

The others all spun to her, frowning at the innocuous bit of blue. LuAnn said, "What in the world is that?"

"A feather. From that one boa, I assume. It's possible it was stuck on one of us when we went in. Or..."

"Or the perpetrator was wearing the boa." Tess nodded.

Leila stepped forward, eyes alight. "We can just check the photos my mom took." She turned her head toward the parlor. "Hey, Mama! Could we see the camera?"

"Or maybe Sophie remembers who had that." Heidi took a step toward the parlor as the two ladies still cleaning up in there stepped out at Leila's call. It only took a moment to bring them up to speed, and soon Marisol was handing the camera to her daughter.

Leila pressed a few buttons and then held it out so the digital screen was visible to those closest to her. She paged through the photographs.

Janice edged closer until she could at least see a glimpse of each picture. Familiar faces, unfamiliar faces, all smiling. Many of them posing. And then there it was. Janice saw the bright boa before she really noticed who wore it. And even then, she couldn't tell who it was. "There it is. Do we know her?"

Heidi squinted at the screen. "I...don't know. She looks vaguely familiar, but I can't think of who it is."

"Mama?" Leila looked up from the camera. "It's photo 1033."

Marisol vanished back into the parlor. "Just a second. Let me get my tablet." She reemerged momentarily, already tapping on the screen of the device.

Janice peered again at the photograph. It was so small on that little screen that she wasn't sure she could have identified the person even if she did know her. All she could tell was that she was blond and wearing a black dress, with that blue boa.

Leila had a bemused look on her face. "That almost looks like Aunt Resa. Doesn't it, Mom? Was she here?"

Marisol blinked. "Theresa? Surely not. She wouldn't dare come to Marietta while Keith is here, as set on avoiding him as she is." She edged up to her daughter's side to look at the screen. "She does look a bit like her, but Resa's brunette."

Leila gave her mother half a smile. "Come on, Mama. Hair dye. Or a wig."

"Yeah, but Resa's...heavy. This woman's rail thin."

"She could have lost weight, couldn't she? We haven't seen her in years. Not since she and Uncle Keith split up."

Marisol shrugged, sighed, and stepped away. She went back to her tablet. "I think it must just be a coincidence, honey. There's no way Resa would come back to Marietta. Besides, according to the photo release, this woman's name is Jackie Simmons."

"Jackie Simmons," Tess echoed. She pivoted for the office. "Almost all our reservations were through the online form. She would have had to enter her address. Let me see if we have any more information on her."

"I think I caught her on video for a minute." Marisol tapped on her screen. "She didn't opt to do a video endorsement, I don't think—only a few did—but I got some B-roll while everyone was moving around. Let me see if...ah, yeah. There she is. Here." She flipped a holder out from the back of the tablet's case and propped it up on the front desk. A tap on the screen started the video.

The woman was edging by another group, a smile in place. "Excuse me," she was saying. "Aren't y'all just having a fabulous time?"

Janice furrowed her brow. The voice was familiar—and so was the thick Southern accent.

Marisol chuckled as the guest waved at the camera, pausing the video when it blipped to the next guest's video mes-

sage. "Definitely not Resa. She's from Boston, not the South."
She flipped the tablet's case closed over the screen.

Leila crossed her arms over her chest, obviously not convinced.

Dempsey rolled her eyes and leaned onto the bar. "Not to hurry things along, but...Heidi, we have a surprise for you! I have reservations at my grandfather's restaurant." She flashed a hundred-watt smile at Heidi. "You deserve a killer after-party after our amazing debut."

Heidi's eyes widened. "Seriously? You guys planned a party for me? That is so sweet!"

The cast gathered around her, their voices all blending together in excited exclamations and their thanks for all she'd done. For a minute, it was just happy chaos as Heidi laughed with her team. Though her grin faded somewhat when she turned back to Janice. "I feel bad leaving without knowing who got into the office. Even worse when I think that it was one of our guests, one way or another."

LuAnn waved away her guilt. "You don't control who buys tickets, Heidi. And this is a business where people can come in at any time. If someone wanted to snoop, they'd have found a time regardless."

"Lu's right." Janice grinned and reached out to grip her friend's hand. "You go and celebrate. You guys did an amazing job, and you deserve it."

Heidi hesitated a moment, but at length she nodded, and her well-earned excitement sparkled in her eyes. "All right. While we change, why don't you download the pictures from the camera, and Mari, can you get that video to them somehow?"

"Sure." Leila's mother was already wandering back toward the parlor, but she flipped her tablet open again. "I'll upload it and send you guys a link."

"That'll be great," LuAnn said. "You can send it to info at Wayfarers Inn dot com."

"Will do." Marisol disappeared back into the parlor.

The actors all headed for the stairs, chattering about this moment and that moment and what they'd do differently next week.

All except Leila, who hung back from the others for a moment, looking as though she was debating something. After a minute, she turned back to Janice and LuAnn and stepped close to them.

"Maybe I'm wrong," she said in a whisper, "but I really think that was my uncle's ex. We've only met her a few times, but she rehearsed a play with me once, and she used that exact accent. I thought it was kind of stupid because the character wasn't Southern. But she said it was the only accent she could do well." Leila shrugged. "If I were you, I'd send the photo to Uncle Keith. He'd know. I don't know what she might have been doing here, but…"

Janice exchanged a glance with her friends. "He mentioned her, I think. I mean, he didn't say she was his ex, just her name. When a woman called the inn who sounded like this Jackie."

Leila let out a slow exhale. "I'm still not sure what happened with them, but I know they haven't talked in about two years. It's weird she'd show up here when he's in town, my mom's right about that. Maybe I'm wrong, I don't know. But if that Jackie lady really is Resa, Uncle Keith would know." She took a step toward the stairs.

"Thanks, Leila. We'll check in with your uncle and get his take." LuAnn smiled.

Janice watched as Leila hurried up the stairs after her fellow actors. The more she was around her, the more Janice had to admit that she didn't seem like the sort to deliberately cause trouble. Circumstantial evidence might still point to her, but she was genuinely trying to be helpful. Maybe...maybe she'd judged her too harshly. Three years ago, and now too.

LuAnn entered the office. "Anything interesting, Tess?"

With a deep breath, Janice picked up Mari's digital camera and took it in with her, handing it to Tess across the desk.

Tess took the camera and plugged it into the computer. "Not really. From what my searching revealed, the address associated with the credit card Jackie Simmons used is just a rented mailbox at a UPS Store in Pittsburgh. Searching her name and that address doesn't bring up anything else. It might not mean anything, or it might mean it was a prepaid card or something. Hard to say." She started the download from the camera and then checked their email. "There's the video. Want to watch it again?"

"Sure. Seeing it on a computer screen instead of a tablet could be helpful." Janice pulled up a chair and made herself comfortable—kicking off her shoes, which were beginning to pinch.

The video started, the woman's sugary voice making her frown again. "That has to be the same woman who supposedly called from the *Columbus Dispatch*."

Tess paused the video after the blonde exited the frame. "She certainly sounds like how you described."

Janice stared at the still image. "When we looked up the number she called from, wasn't it from Pittsburgh?"

"And she asked about the script." LuAnn leaned against the desk, arms folded across her middle. "Did we check the filing cabinet to make sure it was still there?"

They hadn't. But it only took a minute to do so and verify that it was right where they'd left it, with no evidence of anyone having tampered with the lock.

LuAnn sighed her relief. "Good. Still, whoever this woman is, she seems interested in the script, which brings us back to Keith Johnson. We'd better get in touch with him again and see if he can shed any light on why it's important."

Janice agreed. They'd found out absolutely nothing about this woman through their own searches. Maybe Keith would know more.

Tess leaned back in her chair. "Maybe we should pay him a visit tomorrow, if he's free. After church. I'll send him a text."

"Sounds like a plan." LuAnn pushed upright again. "I'm going to go check on things in the kitchen and see if the catering team needs any help or if they're all done. I'll lock that door behind them, either way."

Tess stood too. "I'll tidy up the café, get it ready for breakfast." She unhooked the camera and handed it to Janice.

"I'll give you a hand after double-checking the parlor." Janice brushed a hand over the fringe on her gown as she stood, unable to hold back a smile as it swayed. Despite intruders, it had been a fun night. And she was more than a little bit glad that all the effort she'd put into these costumes hadn't been wasted.

The actors were coming back down the stairs already, garment bags over their arms and laughter on their lips. Sophie and Marisol met them at the front door. Marisol retrieved her camera, and they all went out together.

Heidi waved to Janice. "Thank you so much. Again. I think we got everything, but if we missed anything, just let me know, okay?"

"We will. You go enjoy your party." Janice waved them off, making a mental note to be sure the fog machine and speakers were brought in from the patio. Otherwise, as far as she was concerned, all their stuff could stay put. They'd done a great job hiding it all from sight.

First, though, she did a quick sweep of the parlor. They would just leave all the theater props in place until next week—it wouldn't hurt anything. She would take the costume rack up in the elevator when she went upstairs, but otherwise everything looked to be in order.

Except that stack of half-sheet papers on the table. She went over to grab those and glanced down to see what they were. Looked like a simple survey Heidi had asked the guests to fill out. At the end of the night, apparently. One of the questions was how much they enjoyed the show, with options to circle from one to five. Whether they were from Marietta or the surrounding areas. And how they heard about the dinner theater.

Janice looked at the answer to that last one and pursed her lips. *Saw Leila's video on Facebook.*

She flipped to the next one. *Saw video on Instagram.* Another one mentioned Twitter, again specifying that Leila posted it. She thumbed through the entire stack, letting out a slow breath as the answers added up. Only one sale was from the flyers posted around town. One heard about it on the radio. A couple were word-of-mouth. But almost all the rest saw it on social media, at least half naming Leila as the author of the post.

Janice lowered the papers and stared at the wall. All those photos, the videos she was taking. All that time on her phone. Janice hadn't paused to wonder what she was doing. But clearly she'd been working for the theater, not texting friends or checking her email, which made it highly unlikely she was also responsible for any sabotage.

Oh, Father God. Her eyes slid shut. *Forgive me. I was so suspicious of her, so ready to judge her, so quick to think the worst. And here she's the one they all have to thank for their success.*

It made a strange little ache twang to life in her chest. All these years in ministry beside Lawrence, and still she fell into old habits of assuming she knew a person's story when clearly she didn't. Judging, based on nothing but her own opinions and preconceptions.

Her own hurts. She switched off all the lights but the lamp they left burning in the window all night and padded out to tuck the pile of papers on the shelf under the front desk. She'd left her shoes in the office, but a quick turn of the key she kept with her and she'd reclaimed them.

She turned to the café but hesitated a minute before joining Tess in there.

She'd been offended three years ago when freshman Leila had requested to transfer out of her class, and furious when those machines had been attacked the next day. She'd never really even considered that someone else could have been responsible.

Leila had left her class—that was beyond dispute. But that didn't mean she'd committed the prank. Who was Janice to judge her? Why had she assumed the worst?

She shook her head at herself and whispered another prayer for forgiveness. Goodness gracious goat, Janice certainly wouldn't want to be judged for the decisions she'd made when she was fourteen.

Well. She drew in a deep breath and squared her shoulders, striding forward to help Tess. She couldn't undo her previous thoughts about Leila. But she could do better moving forward.

CHAPTER TWELVE

Janice made a silly face at the baby boy in her arms, laughing when the little one gave her the beginnings of a grin and waved his chubby little fist in the air. She caught it and let little Maxwell swing her arm around a bit.

"My turn." LuAnn wiggled her fingers toward Pastor Ben and Paige's nine-week-old darling. "Come here, Maxwell. Come to Lulu, sweet thing."

Janice relinquished the bundle of love with a chuckle. The sanctuary was emptying out now, but Tess was still talking to Bev Thornton, and Paige hadn't detangled herself from whoever had grabbed her to come and reclaim the baby. Not that they were complaining. And Paige certainly knew that there was no shortage of willing arms at church to cuddle her newborn.

She glanced at her watch—still plenty of time. They'd recruited Robin to cover the front desk this morning during checkout so they could all attend church and then leave straight from here to pay a visit to Keith aboard the *Gilded Palace II*. Keith had been quick to reply to Tess's text last night, inviting them to visit today. According to the email that Leila had sent them sometime during the night, they ought to come between one and two. Keith had invited Leila and her dad to come have lunch onboard and said that the Inn Crowd was welcome to join them.

Another pang of guilt had hit her when they'd seen that this morning. Leila was proving quite a helpful young woman, really. To Heidi, and now to them. No one else had bothered to keep looking for answers about who'd been snooping around their office. A part of Janice still whispered that perhaps Leila was trying too hard, but she squashed that whisper right down. She'd be fair.

The baby started fussing, no doubt thinking it was lunchtime. His cry brought Paige hurrying their way with a smile. "I had a feeling somebody would be getting hungry."

"I sure am. So I guess I'll give you this little prince back so I can go eat." LuAnn grinned and transferred the little one into his mother's arms.

Paige cradled him easily, snuggling him close. Mama looked a little shadowed under the eyes—no surprise with a newborn—and stifled a yawn. "I think my lunchtime might wait until after naptime. When do they start sleeping through the night?"

Janice laughed. "With Stacy, two months. With Stuart... four years."

Paige made an exaggerated look of despair. Or maybe not so exaggerated. "Oh gracious. Four *years*?"

"He was a particularly stubborn little thing. But I'm sure this little angel will be nicer." Janice reached out to brush her fingers over Maxwell's downy head and resisted the urge to add anything more. Any advice not directly sought. It had been hard to learn to let the new pastor and his wife make their own way after Lawrence died, and she wasn't about to slip back into that. Even if the topic was mothering instead of ministering. Paige might not see it as helpful, especially in her tired state.

But Paige smiled and repositioned the baby. "Let's hope so. Thanks for watching him for a few minutes."

LuAnn laughed. "Oh, it was a real hardship. See you later, cutie pie. Happy napping, Paige."

"Thanks." With a bright if sleepy smile, mama made her way up the aisle.

Janice nodded toward the rear of the sanctuary, where Tess was just waving goodbye to Bev too. "Looks like we're good to go." She slid her purse strap onto her shoulder and followed LuAnn toward Tess.

They all exited together, and Janice squinted up into the May sunshine. It was another gorgeous day. Perfect for an outing. She checked her watch again and calculated how much time it would take to get to the dock. "I think we have fifteen or twenty minutes to spare, if we're planning on getting there at one."

"Oh good. That gives us time to swing by Jeremiah's. I've been craving one of their hummus veggie wraps." LuAnn struck out for Tess's car, as she'd been the one to drive today.

Janice grinned. "You read my mind. Except for the hummus veggie part. Chicken cordon bleu sandwich, baby."

"You're both wrong. The Greek salad." Tess fished her keys from her purse and hit the button on the fob to unlock the car doors as they neared.

It only took a few minutes to navigate to the coffee shop and place their orders. They chatted about everything and nothing while they ate and then settled again into the car. Tess drew in a long breath, hands gripping the wheel, before pulling back onto the street. "Here we go."

"I think this calls for a prayer." Janice leaned forward— she'd drawn the short straw on who got to sit where today— and rested a hand on each of her friends' shoulders. "Father God, we thank You that nothing was stolen when whoever it was got into the office and our apartment last night. We put this whole confusing situation in Your hands and ask that You help us get to the bottom of whatever's going on here. In the name of Your Son, Jesus. Amen."

"Amen." LuAnn reached up to pat Janice's hand.

Tess visibly relaxed. "Amen indeed. Thanks, Janice."

Janice smiled and leaned back in her seat. Her gaze swung to the tote bag sitting on the seat beside her, into which they'd tucked the script. Hopefully they'd soon have some answers as to why it held such interest for the mysterious woman.

They had opted for windows down on the drive, and Janice smiled into the breeze that rushed in and danced with her curls. Probably making a mess of them, but who cared? These first warm weeks, before the heat and humidity of summer set upon them, called for some windblown hair and sun-kissed cheeks. Maybe this afternoon she would putter in the garden for a bit.

As soon as they neared the river docks, Janice spotted the *Gilded Palace II*. It was hard to miss, being the largest boat currently at anchor there, its enormous paddlewheel gleaming blue and white at the stern. Pedestrians stared at it as they walked by, some leaning their heads back to take in the gold trim on the stacks.

It was definitely lovely. And appealing. She climbed out of the car without taking her eyes off it. "That is quite the thing. Can you imagine the cost of restoring something like that?" Unless it had been well-preserved, it would surely cost more than the inn's restorations had. And she knew that amount.

Tess rounded the car, briefcase in hand, to join Janice and LuAnn. "Wow. Definitely impressive looking."

Someone waving grabbed Janice's attention, and her gaze focused on the gangway to the boat, where a dark-haired girl stood. Leila jogged down the wide, railed plank toward them.

Janice found her smile came easily to her lips, no shadows of doubt plaguing her anymore. Heidi had been right about Leila—she was a sweet young woman, talented and trustworthy.

Leila rushed up to meet them. "Hi! I guess you got my email."

"We did. Thanks for letting us horn in on your time with your uncle," Tess said with a return smile just as bright and unaffected as Leila's.

Leila laughed. "Are you kidding? He's been gushing all morning about how excited he is to talk to you guys again."

"We're eager to talk to him too." LuAnn led the way onward.

Leila fell in beside Janice with a grin. "I had so many compliments on my costume last night, Mrs. Eastman. Thank you so much. Uncle Keith said he'd get some photos of me before the show next week with his good camera, for my portfolio."

Sunshine warmed Janice's heart. "You're very welcome. You did a great job last night, from what I saw."

Leila chuckled and glanced at the boat. "Thanks. Uncle Keith told me I could tour with them this summer, but my parents freaked at the thought of me being gone this summer since I'll be leaving for college in the fall, so I figured I'd try something closer to home."

LuAnn, half a step ahead, asked, "Where are you going to school in the fall? Have I asked you that before? Not Marietta, apparently."

"No." Leila's cheeks flushed, and she looked down. "I got accepted at Juilliard. Which is so incredible there are just no words. But we're still trying to figure out the money side. If that doesn't come through, my second choice is Barnard—also in New York."

"Wow." Tess sounded every bit as impressed as Janice felt. Those were two amazing, top-notch schools. Not exactly easy for anyone to get into, and not what Janice would have thought of a girl from Marietta spending her summer working with Heidi's start-up theater.

"Yeah." Leila's smile looked big enough to float her to outer space. "I got a decent scholarship at Barnard. It'll still be a stretch, but my parents are pretty awesome. They said if I'm going to pursue the arts, I'll have a better shot at making a living at it if I pursue it at the best possible college."

"That's really impressive, Leila." Janice knew her eyes were still wide as she followed LuAnn onto the gangway. Then she frowned a bit as another thought hit her. "Is that why Dempsey's sometimes so snippy with you? Is she a little jealous?"

Leila lifted her brows, settled them again, and granted the point with a shrug. "I think she's trying really hard to be excited for me, but..." She stepped onto the deck of the boat and pointed to her right. "Down this way, toward the main entrance. The stairs down are in the back of the gift shop." She hesitated a moment, bit her lip, then added, "Hey, Mrs. Eastman...can I ask you for a huge favor?"

Janice paused, no hesitation in her smile now. "Sure. What is it?"

Leila's fingers tangled in the hem of her shirt. "I ordered a dress for baccalaureate online—super cute, but it's too big. Mom and I tried to pin and tuck, but we're hopeless. Do you think, if you had time before Wednesday...?"

"Oh, of course! You can come by whenever you like. Are you all done with school then?"

Leila nodded. "Last classes were on Friday. This week we just have a gazillion graduation rehearsals, baccalaureate, and then the big day on Saturday."

"Wait." LuAnn waved a hand between them. "How are you going to do another show on Saturday, if it's graduation?"

"Graduation's in the morning. It'll be finished by showtime."

LuAnn had a look of horror on her face. "But aren't you having a party or something? Or going to someone else's? You can't spend your graduation night working!"

Leila laughed. "The show is way more fun than a party. But rest assured, my parents and some of my friends' parents already planned a big picnic the next day. It worked out pretty well."

"Leila?" A voice came from one of the doors up ahead, directly preceding the arrival of a man who looked a bit like Keith, a bit like Leila, and was clearly her father. He smiled upon spotting them and held out a hand, to LuAnn first, no doubt because she was nearest. "Oh, the ladies from the inn. I don't think we've officially met—I had to take one of the bumped tickets, so I didn't get a chance to see the show last night. I'm Ian Johnson."

LuAnn shook his hand and then stepped aside so Janice and Tess could do the same. "That's right. And I bet you've heard all about it already, but they did a fabulous job."

"That I did. Hey, Keith, our visitors are here!" After shouting that over his shoulder into the room he'd come from, Ian turned back to them. "Did he invite you guys so you could get a tour of the boat? I know Heidi said she'd suggested working out a deal for discount rates for your guests."

"That's on our list of things to chat about, yes." Janice looked back at Tess and LuAnn.

Tess nodded. "And we'd definitely love a tour. But we have a few other things to ask him about first."

"Well he's certainly excited to have you." Ian stepped back through the doorway he'd emerged from. "Let me go make sure he heard me."

Leila raised a brow toward the ladies. "You brought the video and photo?"

"Yep." Tess patted her tote bag.

"What video and photo?" Keith emerged from the doorway into the sunlight, a big, welcoming smile on his lips. "Hello! So glad you could come."

Leila motioned toward the door. "We'll see the video and photo better inside, out of the sun."

Keith kept on smiling and stepped to the side, holding out an arm, ushering everyone in. "Okay then, inside. After you, everyone."

Janice exchanged a glance with her friends and took up a spot in the little line of people moving through the door. This was it.

LuAnn entered just ahead of her and gasped when they blinked their way into the dim interior. Perhaps this was part of the museum he'd mentioned—it was a huge room, probably the whole width of the boat, and nearly as long. Display upon display of historical items lined it, with a few central exhibits of mannequins decked out in nineteenth-century finery and posed as though they were delivering dramatic lines.

At the far end, closest to the gangway, it appeared to Janice, was a gift shop, complete with a cash register. But this end was clearly more about history. Janice's gaze skittered over a few books and scripts on display behind glass, opera glasses, tins of odd-looking goop, diagrams of what appeared to be theater trap-door systems, rigging...you name it, if it was theater related, it seemed to be here.

Keith squeezed past them and headed for a little alcove tucked into the back corner. "This way," he said over his shoulder.

They followed him past the display items into a stubby little hallway with a door open to an office on one side and a staircase leading downward on the other.

"The theater is on the upper deck," Ian was saying behind them. "There are stairs and an elevator on each end, but of course my brother tries to route everything through the gift shop."

Tess laughed. "That's understandable. Looks like he's got some great stuff. Both on sale and on display."

"I'm sure he'll open the cash registers for you if you want." This from Leila, with a sardonic note to her voice.

Janice focused on following LuAnn and Keith down the stairs. The age of the boat was more apparent here than on the main deck or the gift shop. The stairs were wooden and somewhat warped under their thick paint and treads. Definitely not something meant for guests and paying customers.

It reminded her of some of the places like that in the inn, and it made her smile.

The staircase put them out in a large living area below deck. It was well lit and looked well lived in too, with a kitchen and couches and a big wooden table.

This is where Keith headed. "Make yourselves comfortable. The crew is out, so it's just us here."

"Does your crew live onboard?" LuAnn asked as she hung her purse on one of the chairs.

Keith's smile was lopsided. "More than they'd like to. Our home port is New Orleans, and when we're there, they all just come to work like normal people. We only tour for three months in the summer, and during that time they're in the crew quarters. Which are minimal."

"They do musicals, variety shows, even a special production every year for the kids." Leila pulled out a chair and plopped into it. "I was totally going to be one of the leads in their *Aladdin* production last year, but someone objected." She sent her dad a teasing grin.

Ian rolled his eyes. "Sue us for actually liking our daughter and wanting her home."

Keith chuckled. "And you were going to *audition*, Lei. I didn't say the part was yours."

"To-may-to, to-mah-to." Leila leaned back in her chair with a grin and looked to Janice. "But I imagine the suspense is killing him, despite his cool demeanor. I guess we should show him the pictures."

Janice sat in the chair beside the one LuAnn had claimed, across from Leila, while Tess took the one on LuAnn's other side and opened her briefcase.

LuAnn smiled, a bit tightly, and folded her hands on the table. "I guess Janice should start. She's the one who answered the phone that day."

Nodding, Janice cleared her throat. "Keith already knows this part, but that's where this started." She quickly brought Ian and Leila up to speed, summing up Monday's call with, "I suppose it was in response to that article that came out in the paper about the inn. Marissa mentioned the script. You said you'd see what you could find out about the caller, Keith—anything to report?"

Keith sighed and shook his head. "Unfortunately not. I tried calling and emailing and texting Resa, but—no surprise—she didn't return my messages."

Janice turned to Leila. "Like I told you last night, the woman on the phone had a thick Southern accent, just like the woman's in the video last night. She asked specifically about the script and its connection to the Underground Railroad. We don't have any evidence to suggest it even *is* connected, and we never said we did."

Keith leaned forward, his face blank. "Whoa, wait. Video? From last night?" His gaze arrowed in on his niece. "Resa? Resa is *here*?"

Leila shrugged, her face a strange combination of anxiety and hope. "I'm not sure. Mom said not, but I thought it looked like her. Sort of. And it sounded like that accent she always puts on."

"Here." Tess pulled out the photo they'd printed and her tablet, onto which she'd loaded the video, though she didn't hand them to him. "During the show, someone snuck up to our apartments—we only knew it because the cat got out. Then we noticed someone had somehow gotten into our locked office on the main floor. We found a blue feather in there and matched it to the guest wearing one of the costume pieces. This guest." She slid the photo across the table to Keith.

Keith sucked in a long breath while he stared at the photograph, seemingly set on memorizing every detail.

"Uncle Keith?"

He didn't so much as glance up at his niece. "I can't believe she'd come here while I'm in town. As often as I've tried to get in touch with her, as set as she's been on avoiding me—she must be really determined to see that script." He frowned, looking up now to meet Janice's eyes, then Tess's, and finally LuAnn's. "She's no criminal though. I can't imagine her breaking into your office."

"So..." Leila tapped the photo. "You *don't* think it's her?"

Keith looked down again, yearning shining clearly in his eyes. Whatever had led to the break with his wife, he clearly still loved her. "Oh, it's her. It's definitely her. I just can't quite wrap my mind around it."

Ian, frowning, picked up the photograph. "Wait. This is Resa? She looks nothing like she did last time we saw her."

Keith snorted. "Yeah. It's all part of the 'new her'—the post-Keith makeover, I guess." He looked away, blinking rapidly, but Janice had a feeling the others saw his distress as clearly as she did. After a moment, he turned back to Leila. "Did you see her?"

Leila shrugged. "I didn't notice her during the show or anything. I must have seen her, but I didn't realize it was her. And Mom talked right to her but didn't realize it was her." She frowned. "Isn't that really bold of her? I mean, she had to have realized we could recognize her, and it's not like she didn't know we live here. Or that you're in town."

"Yeah." Keith folded his arms and stared into the space above their heads. "She has to have a pretty good reason to show up here, beyond idle curiosity. And the mention in that article shouldn't have sparked anything but idle curiosity." He blinked and then focused on Janice, Tess, and LuAnn in turn again. "Unless it's just because I'm here. I guess that's possible. That she thought that's why I was in town or something. Not realizing it's really for Leila's graduation."

"But why are you interested?" LuAnn spread her hands on the table. "I don't understand why either of you are so gaga over this script."

Keith sighed with the force of a category-four hurricane and sat down again. "It's... probably going to sound unbelievable."

Tess laughed. "After some of the things we've encountered since buying this inn, our suspension of disbelief is well honed. Try us."

A corner of Keith's mouth turned up, though there was no cheer in his pseudo-smile. "All right. So, Resa and I met in grad school. She was studying the history of the Underground Railroad. I was studying the history of theater. After we got married, we started comparing notes and wondering if our areas of interest ever intersected. The more we researched and discovered, the more interesting the idea sounded. What if theater people were involved in the Underground Railroad? It was surely possible, right? And sometimes we got thinking it was even probable. After all, a lot of theater companies in those days traveled. A lot of them had slaves or free blacks working backstage. Perfect cover for a runaway."

Janice glanced at her friends. LuAnn's eyes were wide with interest, probably caught up in the romance of the idea. Tess would no doubt be thinking more about the practical side of things—the fact that the script could well have belonged to Prudence Willard, who was a known Underground Railroad conductor. For her own part, Janice wasn't sure what to focus on, aside from the obvious. "Did you ever find any solid proof?"

"Proof, no. Nothing concrete. Just bits and pieces. Enough to corroborate our theory but not enough to make it more than just a theory. Still, I started gathering everything I could. Figured I'd write my dissertation on it." He folded his arms over his chest. "And Theresa was thinking the same thing, apparently. We, uh...got in a bit of an argument about who had a right to what research and whose idea it really was."

"A bit of an argument?" Ian shook his head. "You accused her of stealing your work at a party with all her friends."

Keith rubbed a hand over his face. "I was stupid, I know that. And how many times have I tried to talk to her, to apologize? But apparently accusing a professor of plagiarism in public is serious stuff."

"Resa is a professor at a small college in Massachusetts," Ian put in.

Regret etched Keith's face. "We could have gotten past it, if a not-so-nice friend of hers hadn't plastered it all over the internet. She got caught up in defending her integrity, I got kicked to the curb, and all communication has since come through her lawyer." He sent a fierce gaze around the table. "But I did *not* hurt her or her career on purpose. I love her."

"Yeah." The look Ian sent his brother seemed to be thick with emotions he didn't want to give voice to. He cleared his throat. "Didn't she eventually get her doctorate, though?"

"Yeah, two years ago. Wrote her dissertation on the role of women in the Underground Railroad or something. Apparently she had to steer clear of the intersection of the railroad and the theater thanks to the questions I raised."

"But she's still chasing this idea?" LuAnn leaned forward over her clasped hands.

Keith nodded. "It's still her pet theory. Probably in part, these days, just to try to one-up me. She knows I'm still collecting information on it too."

Ian's gaze went to the ceiling, and he shook his head. "Why two reasonable adults who are still in love can't just sit down and have a conversation..."

"Hey, that one's not on me. I've tried." Keith spread his hands wide. "You know I have. I couldn't even get her to be in the same state as me until now. I guess maybe it's time to admit that I'm nothing but a bad memory to her."

Ian lifted a brow. "Then why hasn't the divorce been finalized?"

"What?" Leila gave her uncle a shocked look. "I thought it was! You always call her your ex—you've been separated for, like, three years!"

Keith didn't meet her eyes. "What else am I supposed to call her? I don't know why she hasn't pushed things through, but my hope of reconciliation is pretty thin at this point."

Ian grinned. "Well, if you're looking for a sit-down with her, maybe her interest in this script can prove useful."

Keith chuckled. "Right. We could have her arrested for trespassing, and I could swoop in and post her bail and play the hero."

"With only a blue feather as proof? And nothing even missing?" Janice shook her head with a grin. "Sorry, Keith, but I think you'll need another way to play hero. The police aren't going to arrest someone on such circumstantial evidence."

"To circle back…" Tess looped a finger in the air and reached again into her tote bag. Silence fell when she drew out the script and set it on the table. "I think we need to focus on what it is she's trying to find. And whether it's even worth the effort for her to find it. If this is what she's after."

She slid the script across the table toward Keith.

He reached out with what Janice could only describe as reverence and picked it up. "So this is it?"

Tess nodded. "We haven't found any information on it. So any light you can shed on what it is and if it's really worth anything—monetary or even just interest—is appreciated."

Keith drew in a long, slow breath and flipped through the script.

Leila leaned in, trying to get a glimpse. "Have you even figured out what play it is?"

"No," Janice said. "Our online searches didn't bring anything up."

Keith had turned the script over, and his eyes homed in on the faded inscription. "What about the date? Have you checked local archives to see what might have been in town at the time? Assuming it's from a play that came here, anyway."

LuAnn pulled out her ever-present notebook from her purse and clicked a pen. "Not yet. All our research was online.

But that's a great idea. I can search through the microfilm at the archives tomorrow."

"About that inscription." Janice looked at her friends, and when they both nodded, she continued. "We might know who wrote it. We're not experts, of course, but it looks like the same handwriting as in a journal we have. Written by a Quaker woman who was an Underground Railroad conductor. She used the inn, when it was a hotel called Riverfront House, as a hiding place for escaped slaves."

"Really." Keith looked one part dubious and two parts excited. "A Quaker woman? But they were strictly against the theater."

"Yeah, that's what Marissa said—the reporter who wrote that article." Tess shrugged. "We can't explain why Prudence would have had it or written something on the back. But..."

"But if she did, this might be the best piece of evidence my theory will ever see. She had to have gotten it from someone in the play. And if she kept it, it must have been important." His eyes were practically burning with excitement when he looked up again. "I don't suppose the library with the microfilm is open today?"

"Nope." LuAnn grinned and jotted something else into her notebook. "But today we can try to find a handwriting expert. I don't know if there's anyone locally, but I'm sure we can find someone online and send them scans or something."

Keith gave them a brilliant smile. "If you guys wanted to look on my laptop for that, I'll read through a little of this and see if it rings any bells. I've read a lot of old plays. I mean a *lot*. Before I decided on the abolitionist angle, I'd been planning to write my dissertation on the themes of nineteenth-century drama and how they pushed social change."

"Sure. Though I can use my tablet, if you have Wi-Fi I can sign in to." Tess pulled the device forward.

While Keith provided the password, Janice fingered the zipper of her purse resting in her lap and considered their interaction. All in all, she was convinced that both Keith and Leila were nice people—if a bit overeager on the uncle's part, with trying to sneak a look at the script last weekend. But one question remained in her mind. She made sure the smile she gave him was warm and friendly. "Then afterward, maybe you can give us that tour. I've seen your brochures all around town, and the boat looks amazing. You must have spent a ton of time putting the literature out everywhere." Too obvious?

But Keith barely glanced up from the script, and when he did, it was with a casual smile. "Actually, I only went to a few places. Heidi offered to take them around with her when she was putting up flyers for her dinner theater."

Janice blinked. "*Heidi* did?"

"Mm-hmm. I got the places closest to the dock here, and put up her flyers at the same time. But she outdid me by far. When I called her to report the five sets I'd put up, she said she'd posted twenty-five, and left stacks of them at a bunch of places."

Leila chuckled. "That's Heidi. She sent all the actors with both too, to put everywhere we went."

Janice swallowed, but it did nothing to wash away the feeling of guilt. Yet another time she'd judged someone awry. It hadn't been Keith trying to steal her business—it had been Heidi, trying to be a good friend.

Goodness gracious goat, she had some more repenting to do when she got home.

"Well, they must have worked." Ian folded his hands over his stomach, looking every inch the proud papa. "Lei's show is definitely a hit."

"That wasn't the flyers." Janice spoke softly, smiled softly, and hoped that somehow it would make up for any not-so-nice thoughts she'd entertained. "That was Leila. Her social media posts must have gone viral."

LuAnn nodded. "So said all the questionnaires Heidi had folks fill out last night. She left them at the inn."

Janice had shown them to her friends before they retired last night.

Leila smiled too, her eyes soft and sweet. "Seriously? I mean, I saw that the hits on the videos were pretty high, but that actually translated to sales?"

"Yep." Janice's smile grew.

They still had questions that needed answers. But Leila's loyalty certainly wasn't one of them anymore.

CHAPTER THIRTEEN

May 20, 1851

Prudence stood sandwiched between two farming couples, with barely a sliver of the stage available to her sight. She felt no guilt over viewing this forbidden show. But she also felt no enjoyment. It wasn't ribald—there was nothing morally objectionable to it. But as she watched the actors sweep in and out of her vision, she found herself wondering if they really deserved their trust.

Were they truly abolitionists? Did they really understand the stakes?

At long last, a lanky fellow stumbled onto the stage, his voice quavering as he declared, "Uncle Bean, Uncle Bean! Come quick!"

The main character spun around. "Fiddle! What is it?"

Prudence drew in a deep breath. *Help me, Lord, I beg of thee. Give me a keen memory, to recall every word that is said.*

"The missing money—I saw two fellas burying it, down by the river."

The main character, whose name was Bean, grabbed Fiddle by the arm. "Where? Tell me."

A woman shifted her stance in front of Prudence, putting her hat firmly in Prudence's line of sight. Swallowing a growl lest she not be able to hear over it, she tried for a different angle but could see only Bean's shoulder and ear. Nothing of Fiddle.

Was he hesitating? Or was it Prudence's own anxiety that made it seem so?

"Um…"

A beat of silence, and then she saw Bean's arm move a bit, as if he were shaking the younger man. "Come, lad. Tell me where to find it," he said in a gentler tone.

"You know the twisted oak tree, the one with the lightning strike? Behind the old mill?"

Prudence made it a point to keep her breathing even. She did know it, as a matter of fact. Anna's cousin owned the mill. When Prudence had first settled with Anna, she had spent a few hours at the base of that tree, staring across the river, knowing that if she stepped foot on the other side, she could well forfeit her freedom again. Not that Ohio would keep her safe if a slave hunter came to town. But between her mixed heritage and the Friends, Anna had assured her she would blend in and avoid detection.

And she had. More than three years later, she knew she had. Her looks had changed enough as she came into womanhood that she no longer met the description her mistress would have put out.

"I was by the oak when I saw it. There's a deer path that runs along the river, winding into the forest's edge to the…to the north. If you follow that, you'll come out in a little copse. You know the one?"

Prudence frowned. She hadn't done all that much exploring by the mill. She couldn't have said what deer trails there were.

"Sure I do," Bean said.

"Well, that's where I saw the robbers."

That, then, was where Jason needed to get the runaways.

Prudence scarcely heard the rest of the play. She would have slipped out then and there had she been able to squeeze through the press of bodies, but that might draw too much attention. She waited until the show was over, and the others standing in the gallery all made for the doors. She kept her pace even, matching that of those around her, until she was off the boat and back on the solid dirt of the road. Then, once the night had separated her from the view of the theater-goers, she picked up her pace, until her feet matched her pulse.

It took her fifteen minutes to reach the Jenson farm. Once at the familiar line of fence, she ducked through the split rails and ran across the field—the quickest path to the old barn that sat on the corner of the property, derelict and used only for storing hay. Once upon a time, she'd been told, the original homestead was on this side of the property, near this barn. The original house had burned down decades ago, but the barn had survived—and now would help others survive.

The old doors stood a few feet open, as if the barn had no secrets to hide. She slipped through, into the deeper darkness, and paused a moment to get her bearings.

"Prudence Barton—over here."

She turned at the familiar, baritone whisper and inched her way to the right, not knowing when she might run into something. After a few halting feet, a large, warm hand landed on her shoulder and set it to tingling.

"I am here. *We* are. How did it go?"

"Well enough, I think." She, too, spoke in a nearly silent murmur, swallowing hard when his hand retreated from her shoulder. "I have the directions for thee." She tried to look past him, but the darkness was nearly complete, broken only by the beam of moonlight that had followed her in the door. She couldn't make out who might be behind him, hidden in the hay. Quickly, she relayed the instructions.

She could just make out the uncertainty in Jason's expression. "To the north? Is thee certain?"

"That is what he said. Why?"

He shook his head. "I wish they had chosen a different direction, that is all. The north will put us all but where we crossed the river an hour ago. If…but never thee mind. They are the ones that must maneuver their boat into place to take the boys on board, so they are the ones who must choose the best location. We will make do." His hand rested a moment on her shoulder again. "I thank thee for thy help this evening."

"There is no need to thank me for obeying the Lord." She offered a smile he probably couldn't see in the darkness.

"Get thee home then, back to Anna Barton. She will worry."

She nodded, because obedience had been ingrained into her. But it didn't seem right. Didn't seem to be *enough*. Still, she took a step backward, toward the door. What else could she do? "Go with God, Jason Willard."

She turned, and her fingers curled into her palms. Her feet wouldn't go another step. She couldn't. It didn't feel right. Her blood seemed to buzz in her veins, in her ears, filling her with something she knew not the name for. Dread? Expectation? Warning? Excitement? Anxiety of some sort, to be certain.

Sucking in a breath that did nothing to calm her, she turned again, slowly, to face him in the darkness.

Jason still stood there, looking at her. The hint of moonlight that reached his face told her his brows were arched in question. "Is something wrong?"

"Yes." She lifted her chin. "I must come with thee."

Even the night couldn't hide the immediate objection on his face. "Absolutely not. Thee—"

"It is not for thee to decide." The words came out so strangely. Firm. Resolved. Far more certain than she felt. "I am sorry if I seem willful. But the Lord has impressed this upon me, and I know He would give me no rest if I did not obey. I either go with thee overtly or I follow behind, but either way, I am coming."

He clenched his teeth, his jaw pulsing with the action. No doubt that single speech had ruined any chance she had of

catching his eye romantically. What man would purpose-
fully seek a disobedient wife?

But this wasn't about him. It wasn't about her daydreams
of weaving her fingers through his. It was about something
far greater.

"I haven't the time to argue with thee. Nor to look after
thee as we go."

"I do not require looking after." She said it in a soft voice,
careful to keep any harshness from her words. It was a claim
that would mean nothing until she had proven it, as well she
knew. She began the proof by stepping aside, out of the barn.

Jason released a huff and turned back inside, motioning
with his arm. "Come, my friends. We have no time to waste."

Two boys scurried out of the hay and into his shadow. Or
perhaps she oughtn't to call them *boys*. The younger looked
to be around her own age, and she certainly didn't want
Jason to term her a *girl* rather than a woman. The elder was
probably around eighteen years old. They both gave her a
smile, moonlight flashing on their white teeth.

She smiled back and followed them. If by chance she did
fall behind, she wouldn't hold them up.

It had been years since she'd traipsed through the coun-
tryside in the darkness. More than three years, to be precise,
since it was her own escape her feet hastened along. The
familiar paths took on new characteristics without the light
of day to guide her eyes and feet, but Prudence didn't stumble any more than the rest of them. She kept up with ease,
even though Jason set a brisk pace. Hard work on Anna's

farm had ensured her muscles were firm and strong, and she spent enough time chasing the animals back into their pens that she had no trouble chasing after people.

At last the mill came into view, and the lightning-struck oak behind it. They paused at the base, Jason's head turning first one way and then the other. To the north and then the south.

"What is it?" one of the young men asked in a whisper.

"I don't know where they mean to pull in to the north. It just doesn't seem—but never mind my thoughts. We will follow the directions."

Prudence said nothing, but Jason's uncertainty made her throat tighten. He arguably knew this area better than some showboat pilot who had likely never come this way before, or not more than a time or two, at least. Even so, what good would it do to know the better location if the boat wasn't there waiting for them?

They went north. And with each step, Prudence's chest tightened more.

Perhaps Jason, too, sensed whatever she did. His steps slowed as they neared the place Fiddle's instructions had indicated they should wait, and he held up his hand to halt them. "Wait here a moment," he whispered. "Let me scout ahead."

The two young men hid themselves in the foliage. Prudence simply held her spot, hands balled into fists and pulse still racing.

She prayed. Without knowing quite what it was she prayed for, she prayed. *Please, Father God. Please. Please.*

Jason's steps were nearly silent, at least to her ears. The seconds stretched into a minute, her every sense straining forward, after him. Where was he? To the riverbank yet? Could he see if the boat was where it was supposed to be?

Then a twig snapped behind her. She spun, breath balled up in her chest, ready to fight or fly or whatever she must do to protect those two young men hidden in the bushes.

Fiddle—or whatever the name of the actor was—stood there on the path, eyes wide and mouth open. But before he could speak, terrible noise came from the direction of the river.

A shout. A yell. Running feet. And a gunshot ripping through the night.

Prudence gasped and spun toward the river path, cold certainty in her blood.

They had been betrayed.

Janice wiped the faucet in her bathroom one last time and stepped back to give the sink area her usual once-over. She'd just put out a fresh towel, cleaned the toilet and the shower, and stripped her bed. She scooped up the used sheets and towels and headed downstairs.

On the third floor, she spotted the rolling laundry basket she'd told Robin to leave for her. After tossing her linens into it atop the ones from the third floor, Janice pushed the load toward the elevator. While the ancient machine creaked its way slowly down to the basement, Janice hummed one of the praise songs they'd sung in church on Sunday. The melody had been stuck in her head for the last twelve hours—much longer and she'd have to give in and buy the sheet music for it so she could play it. Sometimes that was the only way to clear it from her mind.

And sometimes it only got it stuck there all the firmer. She smiled as the elevator arrived at the basement and pushed the grate open. There were certainly worse songs to have stuck in her head than one all about the glory of God.

Someone must have already run a load through the washer, because when she opened it up, she found it filled with damp towels. She transferred them to the dryer so she could start the next load.

Resisting the urge to take the lazy way back up, Janice marched herself to the stairs instead, each footfall in time to the music still singing its way through her head. The stairs put her out in the café, already half full of lunch customers enjoying their soup and biscuits and the company of friends. She waved to a few of the regulars she recognized and swung into the kitchen, holding the door open for Taylor, who was on his way out carrying a tray with someone's lunch on it.

"Thanks," he said as he stepped past her with a tip-inspiring smile already in place.

"Sure thing." She let the door fall shut behind him. "Need a hand with anything, Winnie?"

"If you wanted to grab that pan of biscuits out of the oven, I wouldn't object." Winnie was up to her wrists in minced onions.

"I'm on it," Janice said, slipping her hands into the oven mitts waiting on the counter beside Big Red. She pulled the door open, was slapped in the face by the waft of heat, and reached in to grab the two sturdy baking sheets filled with golden biscuits.

She had a jar of strawberry freezer jam left from last year that really needed to be used up. She could practically hear it calling to her from the fourth floor, begging for a biscuit to be put on.

The fluffy golden circles arranged on the cooling rack and brushed with melted butter, Janice turned to find a plate just as Tess gusted in through the swinging door.

Her friend was waving a piece of paper. "We've got a match!"

Winnie raised a brow at her, half a grin nestled in the corner of her mouth. "Trying online dating, Miss Tess?"

Laughing, Tess rolled her eyes at that one. "*Riiiiight.* No. Handwriting results are in." She slapped the paper down on the table.

Janice sidled over to look at the printout. The expert they'd found online and sent scans to had enlarged both samples, put them side by side, and drawn arrows and circles around things that apparently meant something to him. To her, it just made the writing itself hard to read. But she could see the conclusion plain as day beneath the images. "Well what do you know. Maybe we are handwriting experts after all our years of teaching. Our instincts were right. Did you show LuAnn yet?"

"She's still at the library, but I sent her a text." Tess pulled out a chair and sat, gaze on the paper.

"Oh, right." Janice had forgotten that LuAnn had gone to the archive building this morning, after all day yesterday had been spent putting the inn to rights after the weekend rush. They should have known better than to say they'd do anything away from home on a Monday. Her eyes drifted to the biscuits again, still hot and fragrant. "I was just thinking it was time for a lunch break, and the jam calling my name is upstairs. Want to join me up there?"

"Sure. Oh." Tess pulled her buzzing phone from her pocket and tapped the screen, her eyes moving quickly over the text message. "And Lu's almost home, so I'll tell her that's where we'll be, and she can come up to show us whatever she found. You need anything, Winnie?"

"Maybe a spoonful of that jam Miss Janice is talking about." She flashed a wide grin. "The strawberry? I was just thinking I needed another dose of that soon."

Janice laughed. "I'll take a biscuit or two up for you and bring them down liberally smothered."

"One's plenty. Thanks."

"Teamwork at its finest." She headed for the cabinets and grabbed a plate, piling it with half a dozen biscuits. Because she knew her friends well enough to know that if she fixed strawberry-jam goodies for her and Winnie, their mouths would start watering too.

By the time LuAnn joined them upstairs, Janice had prepared and delivered Winnie's treat and was just ready to sit down with her own. Tess had pulled out some fruit to go along with it, and LuAnn had walked in with a tray of iced coffees. All in all, a perfect lunch for a warm May day.

"All right." As the only one with no papers in front of her, Janice figured she might as well play the part of meeting moderator. After taking a bite of the biscuit, of course. Goodness, there was something about the combination of butter and berries that made her tongue dance. "Tess's discovery is pretty concise, so we'll let her go first, then Lu can break out the reams of notes she'll have taken at the library."

"Hey!" But LuAnn grinned and drew out a notebook to set beside her plate. No doubt with page upon page just recently filled.

Tess laughed, licked some jam from her thumb, and pushed her printout toward LuAnn, bringing her quickly up-to-date.

LuAnn sat back in her chair. "Wow. So we now know beyond a doubt that Prudence had a script, which is odd in itself, given that she was a Quaker. She wrote something on the back, which either means it was significant and she wanted to memorialize it…or, I guess, that she only kept it because of whatever she'd written, if it was the note that was important."

Janice pursed her lips. "If it were just the note, why wouldn't she have torn off the back cover it was written on? Especially given how a Quaker would have regarded the theater?"

"True. So, the play itself means something. Which is certainly more interesting for us." LuAnn flipped her notebook open. "Especially given what I found out."

Janice and Tess both scooted their chairs closer to LuAnn's so they could peek at her notes.

"I had no idea what the start of the date was, of course. Just a zero and then 1851. So I just started in January and looked at the tenth, twentieth, and thirtieth of each month. Found some regular plays during the winter months." She tapped her pen on a few lines with various titles written down, and the companies they were being performed by. "In the warmer months, I started seeing showboats and other traveling troupes. This one immediately caught my eye, of course, for obvious reasons."

Janice's eyes widened as she read the line her friend indicated. "*The Gilded Palace!*"

"Whoa. Coincidence?" Tess's brows lifted.

LuAnn shrugged. "Do we know why Keith named his boat after that one?"

"No. Let's ask him." Janice pulled out her phone. "I'll shoot him a text."

"Just invite him to come over when he can, and we'll show him all this." Tess took a sip of her coffee.

Janice reached for her biscuit, eyes still on the notebook, and froze. LuAnn had put her pen down, and the way it covered part of the words on the page... "Wait. Where's the handwriting sample?"

Tess extracted it from under the front cover of LuAnn's notebook and handed it to her. "What?"

"Look. The part under the date—l-a-c-e."

"Right." With a too-patient voice that all but screamed *What's your point?* Tess leaned over to look at where Janice pointed.

Janice tapped her finger to the page, then to the line in LuAnn's notes, partially obscured by her pen. "It could just be a partial word. Part of *palace*. As in, the *Gilded* one."

"Well, look at that." LuAnn blinked and put the sample beside the line of her own script. "You're right. That certainly makes it seem most likely that the manuscript is from that showboat, doesn't it? So it would be..." She moved her pen out of the way. "Something called *The Cache of Kalamazoo*."

"That was one of the character names, wasn't it? Kalamazoo?" Tess asked.

LuAnn's eyes widened. "Why didn't I make that connection? I was just thinking of the city in Michigan when I read it. Well, that makes it seem even more likely."

"We'll see if Keith knows anything about it." Janice typed the question and invitation for him to join them into her phone, praying that soon they'd have answers.

CHAPTER FOURTEEN

Keith and Leila had made themselves comfortable in the common area of the fourth-floor apartment, the glasses of lemonade LuAnn had offered them sitting tall and sweating on coasters. Beside his feet a satchel slouched against the couch. On the arm nearest to Leila, she'd draped the dress Janice would be taking in for her after they talked.

Janice couldn't help but eye it. And then, figuring no one would really care if her hands were occupied, picked it up so she could check out the positioning of the seams and see what fabric it was made of.

"I'd love to say it's some grand story that inspired me to borrow the name," Keith was saying in answer to Tess's question about the *Gilded Palace*. He smiled. "Fact is, I wanted a showboat that originated in Pittsburgh, worked on the Ohio, and had stopped in Marietta, since I have ties here. And preferably one whose owners had never expressed any anti-abolition sentiments. Which is kinda hard to come by, given how many boats spent most of their time in the Southern states. I looked on Wikipedia and narrowed it down to the *Gilded Palace* and one named *Sunshine Buoy*. Frankly, I just picked the one I liked best."

Leila snickered. "You didn't want to be the Sunshine Boy?"

"Buoy." He sent her a mock glare. "And no, I didn't think it suited me."

Leila laughed and peered at Janice where she sat in the adjacent chair with the dress. "Doable?"

"Sure. It shouldn't take too long." She shook out the dress and held it up. "Very cute too."

"So," LuAnn said, her gaze still on Keith, "do you know any more about the boat than what was on Wikipedia? We really couldn't find much of interest when we looked it up. But we certainly didn't dig enough to discover the owner's sentiments about slavery."

Keith shook his head. "Not a ton. I'm actually the one who updated the Wikipedia page, so if you read that, you'll know most of what I do. I'd just also done some looking into the Sullivan family who owned it."

LuAnn lifted her brows, a teasing light in her eyes. "And you didn't create a wiki for them?"

He grinned. "Gotta keep a few aces up my sleeve, right? That, and there really wasn't enough to warrant an article. They emigrated from Ireland a bit ahead of the potato famine, in 1822. Liam Sullivan, the original immigrant, apparently worked at a new playhouse in Pittsburgh. His son was raised there and ended up becoming an actor after working behind the scenes for years. Married a small-time actress, and the third generation of theater-making Sullivans was born. None of them were ever stars, but they must have done pretty well for themselves, to buy that showboat."

"Pittsburgh." Tess leaned against the wall, arms folded across her middle, one finger tapping in thought against the opposite arm. "That seems to keep coming up. The address Theresa gave with the credit card she used to buy the ticket was Pittsburgh. As was the origin of the phone she called us on pretending to be the journalist."

Keith didn't look too surprised about that. "That's where we went to grad school. She has plenty of ties there."

"Well, I say we just need to confront her." Leila pulled out her phone, as if ready to text or call her here and now.

Keith all but lunged for it, snatching it from her hands. "No! You contact her directly, she's going to run. If we want to have a conversation with her, it can't be in a way that has anything to do with me. Last time we were in the same room, she said she never meant to be again. And that woman means what she says."

Leila rolled her eyes. "Chill out, Uncle Keith. If she wants this script as much as you think she does, she'll come and talk to us. She came already, didn't she, even though she knew you were around?"

"Yeah, in disguise." A corner of his mouth pulled up. "She looked good, didn't she?"

Leila let out a snort and grabbed her phone again, though she slid it back into her pocket.

"I think I know how we can get her here." Janice draped the dress over the couch's arm again and reached for their upstairs phone connected to the inn's landline. It would take some scrolling, but the call from the fake Bella Jasper would still be in the caller ID. "This is the number she called when she was pretending to be a reporter. I can just call her back and say we discovered something linking the script to the railroad work—which is true. If you're right about her actions being born of her interest in the script, she won't be able to resist."

Her friends were nodding enthusiastically, but Janice waited for Keith's nod of assent before she started hunting for the phone number. His was a bit slower in coming. And while she was scrolling, he was saying, "She's going to take some convincing. It'll have spooked her to see Mari and Leila."

"Well." There it was, the Pittsburgh area code number from the correct day. "I'm convincing." With a wink, Janice pressed Talk.

The phone rang three times before a feminine voice answered with a rather hesitant, "Hello?"

Janice smiled so that it would come through in her voice. "Hi. This is Janice Eastman of Wayfarers Inn, in Marietta. You called last week?"

"Oh. Yes." Even the Old Virginia mask couldn't cover her surprise. "Did I give you my number? I thought I'd forgotten and was just thinking I should touch base with you again."

"Your number was in our phone." Janice glanced up to meet LuAnn's and Tess's gazes in turn. She gave a small nod, still smiling.

"Oh, of course. That's great. And sorry I hadn't called back yet—following leads and . . . staying busy."

Janice had obviously caught her off-guard. Good. She nearly chuckled. "I'm sorry to bother you, but given the interest you expressed in this last week, I thought you might like to know. That script we found recently, for a play? We've done a bit of legwork and identified it, and we think there is some evidence that it's linked to work with the Underground Railroad."

"Are you kidding me?" Old Virginia slipped into outright excitement.

"Not at all. We'd be happy to show you what we've found."

A beat. A cleared throat. Then, "Could you email what you have, do you think? I—"

"We'd rather not." Janice kept her voice firm but friendly. "Call us old-fashioned, but if we're going to share information about a historical item like this, we'd like to meet you face-to-face. That way you can experience the actual script, and we can get to know each other a little."

On the other end of the line, Theresa sighed. "You're right, I'd much rather see the original than a scan. I can come out there sometime. I don't think I could make it before the week-end though."

"The weekend would be just fine."

Some tapping keys sounded in the background. "I, uh…I see you have an event going on this weekend. I don't want to interfere."

She'd obviously heard Heidi saying on Saturday that there would be a second show—it would take more than a few clicks on a computer for her discover it otherwise. It wasn't as though they were advertising it on the inn's main website. "We do, but that isn't until the evening. You could come earlier."

"All right. I'll make some travel arrangements—"

"You said you were from Columbus, right? At least that's only a two-hour drive." Janice kept her voice sweet as strawberry jam. "And a pleasant one this time of year. Looks like the weather's supposed to have cleared out by the weekend, and we'll treat you to our famous scones and tea when you get here."

"That sounds delightful. Thank y'all so much. Is it all right if I send someone a text when I'm getting close? Will this number work for that?"

"No, this is our landline, but I'll give you my cell." Janice rattled off the number, said her goodbyes, and flashed a grin at the onlookers. "Got her."

Keith was smirking. "And got her good. Might be a two-hour drive from where she said she was, but I know for a fact she's in Boston. That means either a twelve-hour drive or a not-so-cheap flight."

Leila pulled out her phone but just glanced at the screen. Checking the time, probably. Janice knew Heidi had scheduled a rehearsal this evening at the theater, and who knew what else the young woman had to do this week, with all the graduation rehearsals and whatnot.

Janice stood, scooping up the dress. "Shall we?"

"Sure." Leila had a pretty smile, and she offered it freely as she pushed herself up too. "You hanging here or heading back, Uncle Keith?"

"Heading back. Rehearsals to run. See you later, kiddo."

"Bye."

Janice waved to him as well and led the way to her sewing machine. By now, Leila had been in here enough with the rest of the cast that she no doubt knew the drill. Still, she found herself saying, "Go ahead into the bathroom and put it on. Inside out."

While Leila changed, Janice brought out a few spools of thread that might be a close match and the corresponding loaded bobbins for the two that had them. It only took a minute for Leila to emerge again.

Janice smiled. "It's even cute inside out. But yeah, definitely in need of a few darts. Come on over and I'll pin it."

Leila coiled her hair into a messy, curly knot, securing it with a hair band. Too bad that hadn't been the style when Janice was young—she had the curls for it. Not that she'd had her hair long enough for a ponytail in years. She grabbed her pincushion, slid the strap around her wrist, and motioned for Leila to turn toward the window. "Arms up. I'll get the sides first."

Leila obligingly held her arms out to the side. "Thanks again for doing this."

"Oh, it's no problem at all, sweetie. Won't take but a few minutes. In fact, if you can hang out for half an hour, I could just get it to you now."

"You could?" Leila looked at Janice over her shoulder. "Could I . . . I mean, would it be weird or distracting if I watched? I'd love to learn how to do this stuff."

"Really?" Janice paused with a pin halfway to the fabric she'd gathered and met Leila's eyes.

No dishonesty. No teasing. Just a bit of bashfulness as she nodded. "I know I was awful at it in your class—honestly, I was finding several of my classes difficult those first few weeks. Geometry was completely overwhelming me, and it all just felt like too much, you know? So my counselor advised I transfer out of yours—eliminate some frustration. But I've always regretted dropping the class. Especially when it wasn't offered anymore after that year, since you retired."

To keep herself from staring like an idiot, Janice put the pin through the excess material. "I knew you were frustrated. I should have done more to help you. Honestly, I figured you'd get the hang of it any day, but then..."

"Then I quit. And I felt so bad when Trish—" She cut herself off.

Janice looked up now, brows drawn. "Trish?" She searched her mind for the person who belonged to the name. There had been a Trish a year ahead of Leila. She'd had her in class that year too, though she had always seemed more concerned with talking to her friends than actually accomplishing anything in class.

Leila flushed. "I guess with her having graduated last year, I'm not really hurting her by saying anything, but... We were friends, but she was super mad at me over this thing with a guy she liked. It was stupid, but she was mad. And when she heard I was dropping the class, she thought it would get me in trouble if she did something to your machines. I don't honestly know what she did, but she started a rumor saying it was me, and I was called into the principal's office over it. You've probably always thought I did it. I should have told you I didn't, but you wouldn't have had any reason to believe me, and...I didn't want to get Trish in trouble." Her gaze had fallen to the floor during her confession.

Janice drew in a breath and circled to Leila's other side. "I did think it was you. And I'm sorry. I shouldn't have judged you without evidence." She paused and met Leila's gaze. "I hope you can forgive me for that."

Leila's eyes widened. "Of course! You had every reason to think it was me. And I've always felt so bad—I mean, I knew who it was. But then Trish and I made up, and I didn't want to rat her out, and...I still should have, I guess."

"Water under the bridge." Janice smiled and went back to pinning. "So...you still want to learn how to sew?"

"Yeah," Leila said on a sigh. "I've never learned. My mom can sew a button on, but beyond that, she's hopeless. Dad's mom knew how, but she passed away when I was ten. And my aunt, who also knew, has lost her eyesight."

"I could teach you." The words were out before Janice could think better of them. And as soon as she heard them, she knew she didn't want to think better of them. That they were, in fact, the "better."

Leila's eyes widened. "Seriously? You'd do that? I mean, would you have time?"

"Sure. It would only take an hour here and there. And I bet with one-on-one instruction, without the distraction of friends in class and other subjects, you'll pick it up in no time." The seam under that arm finished, Janice moved to the back. Just one more should do it. "You could come here for lessons once or twice a week, and then work on the project at home. Do you have a sewing machine?"

Leila shook her head, looking crestfallen.

"No worries. I have a small one I picked up at a thrift store for a steal. Couldn't pass it up, but I don't need it. Ten bucks, and it's yours."

"Deal!" Leila bounced a little, immediately following it with, "Sorry! Stand still, I know. But this is so awesome! Can we start next week, after graduation? What days? I'm working a few hours a week at my cousin's dry cleaners, but that's only on Mondays, Wednesdays, and Fridays, and then the dinner theater will have practices in the evenings, but…"

"Tuesdays and Thursdays sound perfect."

And suddenly, the summer looked bright and fun.

CHAPTER FIFTEEN

Janice pushed the vacuum toward the honeymoon suite on the second floor, her smile already in place to reassure the harried young mother who stood in the room's doorway, toddler on her hip.

"I am so sorry," the woman said for the eleventh time in the last five minutes since she'd called down to the front desk in a panic. "I really hope it wasn't an antique."

Janice chuckled and wiggled her fingers at the little boy. He buried his face in his mother's shoulder. "Nothing to worry about, I promise." They'd known when they put the pull-out couch in the suite that it would invite families as well as honeymooners, so they'd decorated accordingly. The vase that had just found itself the unfortunate target of a cranky toddler's flying toy car could easily be replaced.

"Are you sure?" The woman—Yasmine Mulligan, if Janice recalled correctly—held the door open for her and her vacuum.

"Absolutely." Upon entering the room, she spied the baby gurgling in a bouncy chair. The little girl couldn't be more than a couple of months old, and she looked adorable in a little pink and white dress, waving a fist in the air. Janice chuckled and detoured to say a quick hello. "Isn't she precious! Look at that smile."

"She certainly is." Yasmine's voice held love, now, instead of apology. Good.

Janice unwound the vacuum's cord. "I'll just get that mess cleaned up so I can get out of your way then." She plugged in the machine and turned to the corner of the room with the shattered vase. In a matter of a few minutes, the mess was history.

Once confident no shards had been overlooked, Janice pulled the plug and headed for the door again with a wave.

"Thank you so much," Yasmine called after her. "And again, I am so—"

Janice cut her off with a laugh. "Not a problem at all. Things break." She grinned at the little boy. "Would he like a few c-o-o-k-i-e-s? We just made a fresh batch. I could send a few up."

The tightness around the mama's eyes finally relaxed, as Janice had hoped. Yasmine smoothed a curl from her little guy's forehead. "I'm sure he'd like that. After his n-a-p."

Janice pushed the vacuum into the hall. "I'll put a baggie outside your door, how about that? You can get them when you're ready."

"That would be great. Thanks."

"My pleasure." Janice turned toward the exit, frowning when something on the floor by the balcony railing caught her eye. "I'm going to vacuum up something in the hallway here real quick too, all right? Then it should be quiet for n-a-p time."

After Yasmine's easy acceptance, Janice let the door swing shut and plugged the vacuum into the outlet between the other two guest rooms on the floor. The mess she'd spotted was close to the fog machine Heidi still had set up there. Something from that maybe? It was hard to say. It could just have been something guests tracked up as they checked in this afternoon.

As she drew closer, the light glinted off it. Glitter. Janice chuckled. Really hard to say when it had appeared, then. That stuff seemed to materialize out of thin air for years after it was used. It could have been from any number of children, or costumes, or certain actresses. She took care of it in half a minute, then unplugged the vacuum again and coiled the cord back up.

Her gaze went from the dormant fog machine to the decorative fabric swag still hanging from the railing. Heidi and crew would be coming over tonight for a quick run-through. Then the show in two days, and then everything would be packed away. It would look a bit strange when all the play's props were gone. She'd gotten so accustomed to seeing them there. Maybe they could make it a yearly tradition, if the business took off as it seemed poised to do. Advertise it on their website as something to draw guests for one weekend in the spring or summer. That could be fun. She'd mention the idea to LuAnn and Tess later.

She stowed the vacuum again and then went down to the kitchen to bag a few cookies. Hopefully the little one liked chocolate chip—didn't everyone? She tucked a few extras in for the parents too, and then ran the treats up to leave outside the door.

The rest of the afternoon vanished in the usual flurry of laundry-folding and storing, café cleanup, and helping Winnie prep for the next day in the kitchen before she disappeared out the back door with a wave.

After a simple dinner of salads and some freshly baked bread, the Inn Crowd was back downstairs as the cast began to arrive for what would be their final practice in the inn.

"You know, I'm going to miss them in the evenings." LuAnn leaned against the front desk as Rand, Scott, and Luke all came in together—on time, no less. "I said as much to Dempsey when she came by earlier."

"Dempsey was here?" Janice greeted that news with raised brows. "When was that? I didn't even see her."

"She stopped by for lunch with a couple of girlfriends. I think you were up on the third floor at the time." LuAnn chuckled. "She gave an impromptu show too. Ran up to the balcony and broke into the famous Juliet monologue."

Janice grinned and watched as the young woman in question breezed through the door, shimmering and glowing as always. And glittering. "Maybe that's where the glitter came from up there. I had to vacuum some up earlier." For whatever reason, Dempsey seemed to think glitter was a staple of her makeup repertoire.

"Seems likely. I've found glitter all over the main floor on the days following rehearsals. She seems to shed it." LuAnn straightened and turned to the stairs, her reception smile in place. "Heading out?"

Janice swiveled her head to see the young Mulligan family coming down the steps, the toddler on Yasmine's hip and the baby in her carrier in her father's hand. They all smiled, and the parents said they'd be spending the evening with the family they'd come to town to visit—a younger brother was graduating high school on Saturday.

"Oh, hey." Yasmine slid close to Janice and pitched her voice low. "Jayden darted out when we opened the door and ran over to the railing. He was fiddling with the swags and one started to fall—I caught it and retied it, but..." Her brows knit. "It's uneven now. I had to tie it up higher, because the cord was breaking. I know Jay is obviously an expert at breaking things, but I don't see how that one could have been him."

"Oh, no, I'm sure not. Unless he's a little mouse nibbling through ropes." Janice held up her thumb and first two fingers, making a nibbling motion to match her sound effects.

Jayden giggled. "No mousey."

His nap had obviously served him well. And maybe the cookies helped too. She grinned. "I'll go check it out. Thanks for letting me know."

"Sure. Sorry we're such trouble."

Janice laughed. "Oh, honey, you are no trouble at all. You guys enjoy your evening with your family, and don't give another thought to that vase. Or the swag."

"You guys are so nice. And the cookies were delicious." She followed her husband and baby out the door.

Janice waved to Jayden, grinning when he actually waved back. Perhaps the cookies had made her a friend. She chuckled and turned toward the stairs. "I'll go check on that swag." It was Heidi's domain, she supposed, but her friend was giving some instructions to Leila and Luke.

LuAnn nodded. "Let me know if you need a hand."

A glance at the draping fabric in question on her way up the stairs did indeed show her that Yasmine's fix had changed its shape quite a bit. Worst case, she'd have to get a new length of twine or something to secure it with. Not a big deal.

But it was odd, she thought as she looked at the ribbon Heidi had used to tie it to the railing. It hadn't just frayed, as ribbon liked to do on the ends. She fingered the thin blue satin and frowned. This had most definitely been cut. She moved to the other end, still in its original position. It wouldn't be for long if left to its own devices. This side's ribbon was cut too, the satin's last remaining strands fraying under the weight of the fabric and ready to snap at any moment. Janice pressed her lips tight together and quickly retied it as Yasmine must have done, raising it up on this side to match the other. She glanced down the length of it.

Something shimmered in the evening light streaming in through the window over the door.

Glitter. A few specks on the swag, on the railing, on the floor that she'd missed.

She pulled in a breath. Dempsey had been up here giving her little impromptu performance at lunch, LuAnn had said. Could she have cut the ribbon?

Janice squeezed her eyes shut. There had been glitter on the fog machine too—not just on the one Thorn had put up as a replacement, but hadn't Janice noticed something glinting a bit on the ground after the original one crashed? And by her sewing machine too, the day the pedal had gone inexplicably missing. She'd thought nothing of it—she had glitter up there for the costuming—she could have spilled some.

But at the moment, it fit a rather telling pattern. Either Tinkerbell was their saboteur... or Dempsey was.

She leaned over the railing to catch a glimpse of the half-dozen actors below. "Hey, Dem, can you give me a hand?"

Dempsey, standing beside Leila, turned to look up at her. So did Leila. She could see that Leila was opening her mouth, probably to volunteer to help with whatever she needed.

Janice half expected Dempsey to let her—but no, she put on a bright smile and hurried up the stairs, the picture of eagerness.

"What do you need, Mrs. Eastman?"

Janice speared her with the same look she'd given her own kids when they thought they were getting away something but most assuredly were not. She pointed to the ribbons. "Any idea why these were cut?"

The question on Dempsey's face looked real—but then, she was an actress. A good one. "What do you mean? They were cut?"

"Drop the act, sweetie." She kept her voice low enough that the others wouldn't hear her and moved her pointing finger to the glitter. "You've left a trail."

Dempsey blinked at the glitter. "Oh. That must have been from lunch. I came up here when my friends dared me to—"

"Yes, I know. But there was glitter under the fog machine too, when its wires were cut. There was glitter at my sewing machine.

No doubt some by the CD player too, had I bothered to look." She placed her hands on her hips. "Care to explain why?"

For a moment, that same blank, innocent, questioning mask stayed in its position on Dempsey's face. But then her expression crumpled, and she looked away. "It wasn't anything that would hurt anybody, okay? Just a few little things to let me prove I could be helpful. I mean, we can't all create viral videos, you know? We're not all going to Juilliard. But that doesn't mean I'm not every bit the actress and team player and—"

"Oh, Dempsey." Janice reached out and gripped the young woman's hands. They had been pretty innocent, all of her pranks. Well, the fog machine could have hurt somebody, but she'd obviously been on hand to make sure it didn't, and then replaced it with her own. "You don't have to do things like that to prove yourself. Being yourself proves yourself. And you are not in competition with Leila."

Dempsey snorted. "Yeah, right. I tried New York for a few months, and I—well, let's just say it wasn't exactly my dream to come back home and take a job with a murder mystery theater, okay? Then to have even that threatened..."

"So fabricating a few minor crises you could intervene in is the answer?" Janice shook her head and squeezed Dempsey's hand. "You want to know what I keep learning over and again? You can't ever prove yourself better than someone else— because you have no control over what they might do. All you can do is you. Be your best you, and keep your heart clear of bitterness. If you let it in, all the acting in the world isn't going to hide it for long."

For a long moment, Dempsey stared at the floor, and Janice couldn't be sure the words were sinking in at all. But then her shoulders sagged. "Are you going to tell Heidi?"

"Are you going to pull these stunts anymore?"

Dempsey's gaze darted up. "I think that would be a really bad idea."

"Yeah, I think you're right." Janice let go of her hand. "Heidi doesn't know the fog machine wires were cut, and I don't intend to tell her. Not about any of it. Not unless I have to, to protect her from future incidents."

"No more. I promise." One side of Dempsey's lips tilted up. "I was out of ideas anyway."

Janice breathed a laugh and nodded toward the cast waiting below. "Glad to hear it. Now you'd better get to work, young lady."

With a silent nod, Dempsey pivoted for the stairs. But she stopped a few steps away and turned back. "What if *me* isn't good enough?"

Was it ever? Janice smiled. "That's when we call on God for help. We can never be all we want to be. But we can be what He wants us to be, with His help. And that is so much sweeter."

She had no idea whether Dempsey had any faith to draw on, whether she had any education in things of the Bible. But she seemed to roll Janice's answer around for a moment, and her nod didn't look dismissive or impatient. It looked contemplative. She moved without another word down the stairs.

Janice held her spot for a moment more, looking out over the café and the part of the entryway she could see from here.

Her own words echoed in her head. They all battled little failures, all the time. They clung to old bitterness, they judged where they shouldn't, they fell back into old patterns. But God was still there, ready to help them be better. Over and over again. Showing them their missteps and guiding them toward His path.

With an easy smile, Janice moved to rejoin her friends.

Chapter Sixteen

Keith flipped through something or another on his phone, nodding. "This must be the flight she was on. Delayed because of a storm. Boston to Pittsburgh, landed half an hour ago. So...it's what, two and a half hours from there?"

Janice snipped the thread she'd been using to sew a massive feather back onto one of the headpieces. Keith had been here for an hour already—only to be greeted with the text Janice had received a few minutes before, saying Theresa had encountered a delay and wasn't "on the road" yet.

Or in the air, as the case more likely was. Regardless, she said she'd text with her ETA when she had it—and just had.

Tess sighed and glanced at the clock. "Yeah. That'll put her here when the play's already started."

Keith sighed. "So much for a simple meeting."

"Well." LuAnn stood, slapping her hands to her thighs as she did so. "You might as well eat with us then. It was my turn tonight, and I have it in the oven as we speak."

Janice swiped her phone from the end table as she stood with the others. Keith was trying to politely object, of course, but Tess and LuAnn would overrule him. For her own part, Janice figured she'd better focus on reassuring Theresa that it was still safe to come.

Because she wasn't happy about the delay, as evidenced by the text that came in even as Janice was ready to tap in a message of her own. *Too late, I know. Don't want to interfere with event. Will come tomorrow.*

Well that wouldn't work—by the time they got back from church, Keith would be at Leila's graduation party, and it sounded as though the outdoor celebration at the park would stretch into the night. Leila had said something about fireworks her dad had bought for the occasion.

She tapped in a reply. *Will not be available tomorrow. You could come in the back tonight and stay out of the way of the event.*

"Coming?"

Janice looked up at LuAnn's voice with a smile. "Yep. Just trying to convince Theresa not to chicken out because of the delay. I told her to come in the back, where she can steer clear of the event."

A reply buzzed in her hand. *Are you sure I'd stay out of sight? Hate to interfere.*

Janice snorted a laugh. "Boy, she sounds so considerate." She keyed in her answer. *Very sure. Text when close. We'll meet you at the back door.*

A brief moment, but not so much that she put her phone away, before the reply came in. *Okay. See you soon.*

"Okay. She'll text when she gets here, and we'll meet her at the back door." Janice pocketed her phone and walked with the others up the stairs to their private kitchen. As they neared it, the scent of chicken and cheese and sauce slithered out from under the door. "Ahh, swiss cheese chicken. I'd forgotten what you were making."

Tess opened the door, scooping up Tom as she did so before he could dart past them all into freedom. Huck yipped a greeting from a few feet back, his tail wagging to beat the band upon sight of a visitor.

Keith obliged the pup with a scratch as he came inside.

Lunch was surprisingly pleasant, given the uncertainty of the meeting to come. They chatted about Keith's boat, his family, the inn, the pets...about everything but the script and the upcoming confrontation with his ex-wife. Those topics didn't seem like dinner conversation to Janice, and the others must have agreed. Keith volunteered to wash the dishes afterward and nudged Janice out of the way at the sink before she could object.

She surveyed him up to his elbows in bubbles a minute later with a smile.

"There's the first of the cast," LuAnn said from where she stood by the window. "I'll put the critters away. Come here, Tom." She bent down and made eye contact with the cat, who took his sweet time in obeying, winding first around the legs of the table and two of the chairs. But he came—he always did when LuAnn called. Eventually.

Huck followed her without any need for a command at all.

Janice loaded the last of the plates into the dishwasher. With only the pans and serving spoons to wash by hand, Keith and Tess wouldn't take long. "I'm going to go check my sewing room and make sure it's ready to become the dressing room again, then change." And then lock her doors. Tess caught her gaze, obviously hearing the silent addition. "Be back in a few."

By the time Janice had tidied up a few items she'd forgotten to put away earlier, she could hear the banter of the cast as they came en masse up the stairs and through the door, calling out greetings to the two in the kitchen. She stepped into the doorway to welcome them in, exchanging warm smiles with both Leila and Dempsey. "Everybody ready for your encore performance?"

"Ready and eager." Dempsey stepped into the room.

Janice angled her smile to Leila. "How was graduation?"

"Long and boring, but hey. I am officially a high school graduate, so no complaints." She glanced toward the kitchen and dropped her voice. "Uncle Keith texted to say she wasn't here yet. Everything okay?"

"Flight delayed, apparently. Not that she said as much, but we're assuming. She should be here in ... " Janice checked her watch. "An hour and a half. She'll be coming to the back."

"After the show, I want a full reenactment of what happens." Grinning, Leila sidled past on her way into the dressing room.

Janice chuckled. "I'm sure you'll get one."

She moved fully aside to let Leila in and took herself into her bedroom to retrieve her costume. After changing and then locking up behind herself, she ducked into the dressing room and met Heidi's eye. "Hey, do you want live music for the pre-show again, or your CD?"

"Oh, I don't want to impose. We can use the CD." Heidi jabbed a pin into her blond finger waves.

"It wouldn't be an imposition. You know how I enjoy playing." Frankly, it would help dissipate some of the stress from waiting for Theresa, though she had no intention of getting into all that. "But if you prefer the CD—"

"I certainly don't *prefer* it." Heidi laughed. "Live music always trumps recorded—well, at least when it's good live music, which yours certainly is. If you want to play, I'd love it. But if you have other things to do, please don't feel obligated."

"I would be delighted." Janice reached over and squeezed her friend's arm. "I'm so glad this is going well for you, Heidi. I can't wait to go to one of the next shows you do, if you keep having a few public options."

Heidi beamed. "I think we're going to eventually try to do one or two a month at the People's Bank Theater. They're obviously booked right now, but I managed to fill a gap at a smaller place. Next few will still be Mafia themes, so we can use the same costumes, but when we switch eras..."

"You know where to find me, and the friends and family discount I gave you on my rates will still apply." Janice made a shooing motion back toward the mirrors and trays of makeup and racks of costumes. "Go get ready. I'll see you later."

After letting Tess and LuAnn know she was going down, Janice headed for the piano. She'd been reading her Bible every morning as usual, of course, and praying, but music was always one of her favorite ways of communing with the Lord. Even when the songs in front of her weren't strictly spiritual—

as would be the case with the sheet music she'd pull out—she would often write her own words of praise and supplication as she played, singing them silently to God.

She could use some of that communing now, before Theresa arrived. Setting her phone on the bench beside her so she'd feel the vibration if the woman texted again, Janice got comfortable.

Since she had bushels of time before any guests or even helpers like Marisol or Sophie would be arriving, she started by pulling out one of her favorite books of worship music, to get herself in the right frame of mind. These particular arrangements of old, familiar hymns combined the melodies she'd grown up hearing with new riffs and flourishes to make her soul sing as her fingers danced. She played and prayed her way through her two favorites and then switched to the twenties-era music when she glanced at her watch and realized the time had sped by, and the two helpers were already set up on the other side of the room.

The evening wheeled by much as last Saturday had. The guests once again laughed their way into costume, had their pictures taken, and took their seats until the café was full. No new texts came in before the play began, nor before she, LuAnn, and Tess did their big number, to the applause of all. It wasn't until they ducked into the kitchen during the intermission that her phone buzzed.

"Perfect timing." Janice motioned for the others to follow her toward the back door. They signaled Keith to join them, though he'd stay back out of sight while they greeted Theresa.

He'd watched the first act of the play from the café, and he was still smiling.

Please, Lord, let that set the tone for this. Give us Your wisdom and discernment, and help us to see this situation through Your eyes and not our own. She'd done enough judging of people these last few weeks without really knowing what their story was. She didn't want to be guilty of doing the same with Theresa, despite the evidence stacked against her.

She opened the door to the cool spring air. A few seconds slid by with only the chirping of frogs—the first she'd noticed them this year—and the echoes of laughter from other parts of the inn filling the night. Then came the click of heels on flag-stone, and a woman emerged from the night.

Janice's brows nearly went up, but she schooled her features just in time. This woman didn't look much like the one who'd bought a ticket to the show last week—the long blond hair was gone, and in its place was a stylish short bob in some dark shade. Her face was the same though, Janice confirmed as Theresa stepped into the circle of porch light. The same smile. And she'd obviously come ready to blend in tonight if the occasion demanded it—she wore a drop-waist dress.

Janice wondered idly which hair was real and which the wig. Was this the actual Theresa, or was she just trying to look like Bella Jasper, in case they had looked her up? Janice hadn't done that—but now wished she had, so she would know.

"Hello," she said with a smile of her own, holding the door open. "So glad you finally made it."

"Me too—I am *so* sorry for the delay." Southern accent thickly in place, Theresa stepped right past her into the hallway. "You sure we're not in the way?"

"I'm sure." Janice shut the door behind Theresa and stayed there, between Theresa and escape. Not that she wouldn't move if Theresa asked, but when she spotted Keith, she might just need a visual deterrent to convince her to hear him out.

"What in the world—?" She'd obviously seen Keith. And she did indeed spin immediately back toward the door.

Janice held her ground in front of it, hoping her face showed grace and sincerity. "Just hear us out, Theresa. Please. Listen to us, and then we'll show you the script."

"Resa." Keith stretched out a hand toward her, his fingers begging for hers. He sounded...well, like a man desperate to talk to his wife. "Please don't just run again. Maybe you don't owe it to me, but you owe it to these ladies, don't you think? They know you were here last week, they know—"

"You don't know anything." The accent was gone, panic in its place. Theresa pivoted back to face him, poking a finger into the air in his general vicinity. The finger shook, and her expression flickered too. "And I'm not talking to you. If they're on your side—"

"We're not on anyone's side." Tess held out her hands, imploring. "But I certainly would like to know why you broke into our office last week."

"And why you've lied about who you really are," LuAnn added. She raised two fingers. "Twice. I mean, really, if you wanted to ask us questions, why in the world didn't you just tell us your name and ask?"

Theresa folded her arms over her chest and lifted her wobbling chin. Her mask of toughness and anger was quickly dissolving, her eyes misting. "When he's already in town? Yeah, right. I know very well he'll have already offered you any price you asked for that script."

"Actually..." Janice grinned. "He only offered us fifty, and even that put us on the defensive."

Keith let out a huff of mock outrage and grinned back at Janice.

Theresa shook her head. "Right." Dropping her arms, she gripped the bag slung over her shoulder and edged past the others, toward the lobby.

"Resa!" Keith surged after her. "Come on, hear us out. You know you want to see the script. Isn't that worth a few minutes of suffering in my company? Don't just run away again."

"Oh, boy." Tess ran after them.

She must be thinking the same thing Janice was—that had not been the best thing for Keith to say. "Goodness gracious goat." She hurried after them too, LuAnn falling in behind.

Theresa was charging into the lobby, shouting over her shoulder, "Why should I stick around? So you can try again to ruin my life?"

"I was not trying to ruin anything—I said something stupid, and I've paid for it, haven't I? I lost the only thing that mattered. *You.*"

Theresa halted by the front desk, her fingers gripping the straps of her bag. "You're not going to sweet-talk me, Keith Johnson. I know very well you've still been seeking any evidence you can find about—"

"Yeah. I have." He circled around to stand in front of her, eyes blazing. "And have you ever paused to ask why? So I can hand it all over to you. Make up for my stupidity, if I can."

Her nostrils flared. "Yeah, right."

Keith had donned costuming for the night, which hadn't been any great surprise for a theater owner. But as Janice watched them square off there in the middle of the lobby, guests watching with wide eyes and clipboards at the ready, she had to smother a laugh behind her hand. "They look like part of the show," she murmured to LuAnn.

LuAnn grinned. "I daresay the guests think they are. Look—those two are taking notes."

From a step ahead of them, Tess chuckled. "Let's get them somewhere else before we have a genuine murder to be solved though, shall we?" She moved again while Keith replied with something Janice didn't hear, but which didn't seem to soften Theresa any.

Janice shook her head and trailed Tess to the couple.

LuAnn beat her there, and Janice didn't have to see her face to know there'd be a spark of fun in her eyes when she said, "All right, you two. We don't need any domestic spats in our fine establishment." Her imitation of Rand's gangster voice was, of course, spot-on.

Tess was already unlocking the office door and flicking on the light. "In here. Quickly." Her voice also held a lilt, as if she were delivering lines.

Still, Theresa clearly wavered, glancing at the front door with apparent longing before seeming to decide that the allure of the script outweighed that of escape. Eventually she sucked in a breath, lifted her chin, and strode into the office. Keith followed.

Phew boy. With a wink for Leila, who still stared with wide eyes at where her uncle had been a second before, Janice brought up the rear of their quintet and let Tess close the door behind her.

"All right. Would you like to sit down?" LuAnn pointed at two of the three chairs.

Keith sat. Theresa didn't. She took up a position by the desk and gripped her bag with white knuckles.

Instinct, or did she have something in there she didn't want Keith to see?

Janice sighed. She'd seen her fair share of estranged couples over the years. And since that might give her a wee bit more experience in how to talk to them, she stepped forward. "Okay. First of all, thank you for hearing us out, Theresa. I know it's difficult for you to be here with him."

Keith gave her an indignant look.

Theresa shifted from foot to foot. "I'm not doing it for him—but he's right that I owe you an explanation and an apology."

"Thank you—I know we all want to hear what you have to say." Janice smiled, moving it from Theresa to Keith. "For the moment, can we take a step away from your personal history? Let's focus first on the script you were both so eager to see that you resorted to lying."

She arched a brow at Keith, who had the good sense to look sheepish and drop his gaze. When she moved the reproach to Theresa, she was surprised to see the woman blinking back tears and gripping her bag even tighter.

"First, let me say I'm sorry about last week. I didn't *break* in, I just happened to see her"—she nodded to Tess—"lock up and slide the key onto the top of the doorframe, and I...I just wanted a look. I wouldn't have hurt anything, and I wouldn't have taken anything, and I still can't believe I actually had the gall to do it."

Tess let a breath slip past her lips. "I knew I should have carried my keys that night rather than use the spare. But they wouldn't fit in my costume pocket."

LuAnn patted Tess's arm. "We've all done things like that. And no real harm was done." She lifted a brow and looked at Theresa. "I guess."

Theresa's cheeks were stained pink, and her shoulders hunched. "I don't know what got into me. I was just so panicked at the thought of Keith getting it first—I was wrong. I realize you probably need to report it to the police. I'll cooperate."

Should they believe her contrition? She looked to Keith again. "How good an actress is she?"

Keith pressed his lips against a grin. "Awful."

Dragging in a long breath, Janice exchanged a glance with her friends and, at their nods, looked at Theresa again. "We're not going to call the police. No harm was done, aside from our cat getting out—assuming you were the one who went upstairs too?"

Theresa flushed scarlet.

Answer enough. "Okay. No harm, no foul. You were looking for the script? The one you'd called about, pretending to be a reporter?"

A jerk of a nod.

Janice looked to Tess. Tess slid over to the filing cabinet and soon had the bound papers in hand. "Keith has already seen it," Tess said. "So it's only fair you get to as well." She winked his way. "He tried to sneak his way in here too, actually. You're obviously both very passionate about this theory of yours. So how about we all work together here? If we compare notes, then we'll all be on the same page and no one can scoop anyone else. Okay?"

Keith nodded. "I don't want to scoop her anyway. I wanted to give it to her."

Theresa shifted her gaze away from him and crossed her arms over her chest. But it didn't look defiant so much as defensive. "Sure. That's easy to say, Keith."

"I'd prove it, if you'd give me half a chance." With a sad shake of his head, he offered a weak smile to Tess. "Go ahead."

Tess held the script out to Theresa.

For a few seconds, the younger woman didn't take it. She just stared at it, seemingly with a million thoughts twirling through her head. Then, rather than reach out, she reached *in*. Into her own bag. "Oh, wow. I think...I think it's..." And then she pulled out...

Another script. No, the same script, from the looks of it. The same faded blue cardstock cover, the same yellowed pages, the same size. She held it out, and Tess took it, fitted it to the half in her own hands.

A perfect match.

"Where did you...?" Awe filled Keith's tone, tinged by incredulity. He scooted his chair closer, his gaze also on the now-complete script in Tess's hands.

Theresa didn't make any motion for him to move away again. She was too busy staring too. "Where did *you*...?"

LuAnn motioned toward the door, then the inn at large. "It was in a box of old books from the original hotel. Hidden. We can only assume that it was hidden by Prudence Willard, a conductor on the Underground Railroad. Her handwriting is on the back of our half."

Tess handed the bottom half to Theresa, back cover up.

Theresa traced a reverent finger over the torn-off inscription. "Do you know what this indicates?"

"The date the play was performed in Marietta, from what we can tell. And we had an expert verify that it's Prudence's handwriting." Tess lifted her brows. "Where did you find the other half?"

Theresa still looked half in shock. "Toronto."

"Toronto?" Keith leaned forward, eyes glinting. "Where? How? What did it—?"

Theresa laughed, and Keith jerked back upright as if he'd been zapped by lightning. He definitely still had it bad for his estranged wife, and the animosity had vanished from Theresa's gaze when she looked at him. Maybe there was hope for them yet.

Janice said a silent prayer to that effect.

Theresa wiped what must be a happy tear from her eye. "Well, I'll tell you what I know."

CHAPTER SEVENTEEN

May 20, 1851

"Wait!" A hand gripped Prudence's arm, the urgent whisper stilling her more than the touch. "Don't rush headlong into danger. Are they down there already? The boys?"

She wrenched her arm free. "Thee thinks I will hand them over to thee? After what thee has done?"

But the actor shook his head, his eyes wild. "You don't understand, miss. I—I flubbed. My line. My mind went plumb blank, and I—I meant to say south, not north. And my father, he didn't realize what I'd done, because I was the one doing the scouting this morning. Not until he pulled the boat away from the dock and headed downstream, following my directions. That's when I realized what I'd done. Please, miss. You gotta believe me."

Maybe. But she couldn't even think through that question right now, she couldn't be sure he wasn't part of whatever was happening at the riverfront. All she knew was that

Jason's life was in danger right now, more so with every shout. She backed up a step. "I must see what has happened."

She also must do what she could to help these young men. Could she trust this actor? Did she dare? She didn't know, and the urgency in her chest only pushed her toward the river.

She shook her head and motioned to the trees to the right, on the opposite side of where the brothers had hidden. "Wait here a moment. I will return directly."

Without waiting for his response, she pivoted again and took off at a run. Her feet didn't stumble now over tree roots or downed branches. It seemed to her that they fairly flew along the path, silent and fleet.

She halted just before leaving the tree line, when voices carried through the night and found her ear.

"Where did he go? Did you see him?"

"He's gotta be around here somewhere."

Prudence sucked in a breath without making a sound. She didn't recognize the low voices, but she had to assume that Jason was the "he" they were looking for. He must be hiding somewhere near here. How could she help him without giving him away?

For an infinite moment she debated, praying fervently for an answer.

Movement to her left caught her eye. The twitch of an ear. A deer, frozen perhaps ten yards away, obviously as wary of the intruders as she was. Peace lit upon her heart. God had sent Abraham a ram, providing the sacrifice. He had just sent her a doe.

Bending down slowly, she picked up a rock half-buried in the dirt of the path. *Lord*, she prayed silently, *make my aim true and give that doe Thy wings, that it may soar like an eagle and lead those men away from Jason.*

She let loose the rock, aiming it toward the deer. As she had hoped, it started and ran in the opposite direction, charging through the woods with the same thrashing that a man might make if he'd given way to desperation.

"There! Hurry!"

Two loud pairs of footfalls followed the deer. Another shot rang out, but the deer's noises continued onward, as did the steps of the men.

Prudence finally dared to breathe. "Jason Willard!" she called out, softly enough that it would be audible only to someone a few feet away.

A groaning "Here" came in answer from just a step away.

She hurried into the brush, only seeing the boot half a second before she would have tripped over it. Crouching down, she pulled the brush away and caught her breath when the moonlight revealed a blood-soaked leg. "Jason! What has happened to thee?"

"Shot." A hand entered her vision, bloody and dirty. "Help me up. We must hurry before they come back."

"Thee cannot stand on this leg!"

"I have little choice."

Given the truth of that, she gave up arguing and instead gripped his hand. It took them an impossibly long time, but eventually he was upright and moaning in clear agony, his hand clutching his thigh.

It looked far too dark and sticky in the moonlight. Her heart raced from more than the exertion. "We must hurry and get thee to Dr. Williams."

"No," the fool man said from between gritted teeth. "We must complete our mission."

Prudence shook her head, gripping him around the waist when his strength failed, and he sagged against her. He was heavy—too heavy. God would simply have to give her the strength to help him.

"Please," a new voice said from the path. "Let me help."

Fiddle. Prudence caught her breath and had little choice but to help Jason stagger a step toward the stranger, given his lunge in that direction. "It is the actor," she murmured. "The one playing the role of Fiddle."

"Virgil," Fiddle said. He held his hands out palms up, demonstrating, she supposed, that they were empty. "Virgil Sullivan. Please. I've ruined everything, and I am so sorry. You're injured?"

Agony laced Virgil's voice nearly as heavily as it had Jason's. But how could they trust him? This man made his living telling lies convincingly, after all.

Jason's arm had settled around Prudence's shoulder. Necessity, not affection. She was naught but a crutch, and she well knew it. How she wished it weren't necessary. She helped him another step.

To Virgil he said, "What is thee doing here? The plan was—"

"The plan was ruined by my mistake. When I realized it, I knew I must make amends." He motioned toward the north, where the thrashing had gone. "Those men?"

"From a plantation across the river." Jason cut himself off with a heavy breath, clutching his leg. He squeezed his eyes shut.

"My friend." Virgil edged closer. "Please. Let me help. If you do not trust me to lead the lads to safety, then at least let me support you to the doctor. I am stronger than she is."

Prudence stood up taller under his dismissive nod.

For a moment, Jason was utterly still. Then he opened his eyes again and shook his head. "No. Thee should lead them to thy boat. It is the best use of time. And then hasten away, before those men realize what we are about. Prudence Barton can get me to safety."

Jason trusted him? Even now, with his leg bleeding because of this actor's blunder?

Virgil loosed a gusty exhale. "I thank you for your faith, when it surely seems ill earned, I know. I promise you, I will never blunder in this way again. Father is always after me to learn my lines better. Saying improvisation has its place but isn't to be relied upon."

"Well, we will improvise now." Jason nodded and then whistled like a nightingale.

The brothers emerged from their cover.

Virgil looked behind him, seemingly amazed to realize they'd been but a few feet from him the whole time, and then turned back to Prudence and Jason. He moved forward, first digging around in his pocket and then holding out his hand. "Here." He indicated the pocket on Prudence's apron and slipped something heavy into it. "For the doctor's bill. My cut from tonight's performance."

The action put his face so near hers that she could see into his eyes even in the dim light. Not their color—but their character. She saw the earnestness in them. The sincerity. The need to be trusted, to be believed. To help.

She nodded, shifted, and the coins jingled a bit in her pocket. "I thank thee. Now hurry. And Godspeed."

Virgil looked again toward Jason, his expression torn. "I will make this up to you. Somehow, someday. That you should suffer for my mistake—"

"Just go. Quickly." Jason attempted a smile, though it looked more like a grimace to Prudence's eyes. "We all make mistakes."

Without another word, Virgil spun and led the way back along the path at a jog.

Prudence gripped Jason tighter when he sagged. "Come. If we can get thee to that rock we passed, thee can wait there. I'll fetch the miller. He will help us to the doctor's."

But rather than move with her, Jason stayed rooted to his spot, which made her cast her gaze up at his. He swallowed. "I am glad thee insisted upon coming, Prudence Barton."

She dug up a bare smile. "So am I."

"What I know is that this was with the belongings of a modestly successful playwright. Oswald Green." Theresa drew out a few photographs from her satchel and set them on the desk. Her gaze drifted over to Keith and caught his. "I figured I would chase our theory from the other side and started researching any reference I could find to black men or women in the Canadian theater during the right stretch of time."

Keith's mouth curved into a smile. "Smart thinking. Bet there weren't all that many."

"Not recorded, anyway. Stagehands—I saw some photographs—but they weren't generally mentioned in any documentation. But then I found Mr. Green." She pulled out a few more stacks of paper. "He wrote a few plays in the late 1850s and early to mid-60s, all painting slavery in an evil light. Made me think he may have had a personal stake in the subject."

Janice edged closer to peek at the items on the desk. The stacks of papers appeared to be copies of a couple of the plays he'd written. She read their titles—*A Little Bit of Mercy* and *Virginia Boy*—and looked at the photos she'd laid out. They seemed to be snapshots of display cases, the sort found in museums. She could only make out the vaguest impression of photographs within the photographs, of a tall African man in a black suit. A man with a woman, then another with children on the laps of the adults.

"Have you found any evidence that he escaped from slavery?" Keith picked up one of the plays and flipped through it.

"Hints. But nothing concrete until I found this." She motioned to the top half of the script. "It wasn't out on display—

the curator said it wasn't worth displaying, so he let me buy it. Look inside the cover."

Since Tess still held it, she obliged, and they all crowded in. Janice couldn't see the whole thing, but the scrawl she did see was enough to tell her it wasn't Prudence's handwriting.

Tess softly read, "'To Oz, so you never forget the path that led you to freedom. Sorry for the bumbling. Fiddle.' Fiddle?" Tess looked up with a frown. "That's one of the characters in this play."

Before Theresa could answer, Keith jumped in, grinning like a little kid. "It is. I did some looking once we had the title and knew it was performed on the original *Gilded Palace*. The part of Fiddle was played by the son of the family who owned the boat. Virgil Sullivan."

Theresa leaned forward in her seat, straining toward Keith. "Where did you find that? I've been trying for months to find any mention of this play, and I kept coming up blank."

Could she resist the grin he sent her? Janice was none too sure, especially given the way she grinned back.

"Well," he said, "I guess that's because you weren't looking in *my* museum. I'd gathered anything I could find from the original *Gilded Palace* when I decided to name my boat after her. I had a journal in there—bought it from an estate sale because it had a postcard of the boat on the front. Turns out it was written by one of the Sullivan sisters. She didn't say much, mind you—it was just a log, basically, of the ports they docked in and the plays they performed, the number of attendees, that sort of thing. But it told me that much."

Theresa scooted to the edge of her seat. "How much of it did you look through? Is there any mention of an Oswald or Oz anywhere? Did he join their cast or crew?"

"Well, I don't know. Let's see." He got up long enough to retrieve the satchel he'd stowed in there earlier. Apparently he'd come prepared with his own notes too—including an old, beat-up looking leather booklet with the postcard he'd mentioned on the front.

Janice blinked at it and looked up at Tess. It reminded her just a bit of the journal they'd found hidden here. Written by Prudence.

Maybe Tess was thinking the same thing, because she spun back for the drawer in which she kept her printout of the scanned journal.

LuAnn watched her too. "You know, I keep thinking that if this was something that involved Prudence, it would have had to be one of her earliest missions. She wouldn't have been much more than a girl."

"And she didn't start keeping a journal until five years later—well, assuming this is the first journal." Tess pulled out her pages and leaned against the desk, flipping through. "But I think, now that we have some information... Here." Excitement lighting her face, she flipped the earlier pages over to reveal just the one she'd been looking for. "There's one from May 20, 1861 that might be relevant."

Janice frowned. "That's ten years later."

"Exactly." Tess grinned. "Exactly ten years later. Listen. 'Today a most unexpected visitor stopped by the farm and took a meal with us. We have not seen VS for a decade. And oft were the times we wondered whether he was friend or foe.'"

"VS." Keith held out a hand toward Theresa, his gaze on Tess. "That could be Virgil Sullivan."

Theresa gripped his fingers in hers. "It could."

Janice bit back a grin and nudged Tess to continue.

Tess obliged. "She says, 'How easy it is to let conviction become pride. But how rewarding it is when we hear the whisper of Thy sweet, still voice in the midnight and finally stretch out a hand and find it grasped by the fingers of a friend. That is how we feel now, looking back and realizing how surely Thee led us that terrible night. The night my sweet Jason could have died for freedom's work. The night I first tasted what it truly was.'"

"I wonder what happened that night." LuAnn's gaze was distant, misty, the way it always was when she was caught up in a story in her own mind.

Tess dropped her gaze back to the journal copy. "She doesn't say much. Just that Jason was shot in the leg during a delivery—that would be their code for an escape," she added for Keith and Theresa. "And that for so long they'd wondered if it had been betrayal or happenstance. Here she says they rarely ever knew where the packages—that would be the escaping slaves—ended up, and this time they hadn't even known their names. Until V told them that O and J arrived safely in the north."

"Canada." Theresa was gripping Keith's hand so tightly it must hurt. Though he was grinning, not wincing, so who knew? "Oswald, and his brother, Jemmy. They were here, Key. They were slaves, and they escaped, and they must have been helped along somewhere by Virgil."

Keith was nodding enthusiastically. "They may have even worked on the *Gilded Palace*. It would make sense, wouldn't it? That's how Virgil would have known where they ended up. And it would explain Oswald's presence in the theater world. Otherwise, what could have drawn him to that?"

Theresa squealed, the sound muted but clearly delighted. "We were right, baby. We were *right!*"

Tess sidled away as they threw their arms around each other, laughing and hugging. Her grin looked every bit as indulgent as Janice's must. They huddled together where LuAnn stood.

Janice glanced to the two halves of the script sitting on the desk. "You know, it seems only right that the two halves be united, doesn't it?"

Her friends grinned.

"It does. Tess?"

"If they agree not to fight over it in any divorce proceedings." She chuckled, since that certainly looked like a bit of a joke with Keith and Theresa wiping each other's tears away and laughing.

"Ahem," Janice said, loudly enough to gain their attention. She arched her brows at them. "Are you two going to work together on this again?"

Keith looked at Theresa. "I don't know. Can you forgive me, honey? Can you believe I never meant to hurt you?"

Her expression softened. "I know you didn't. I was just so mad at the blow it dealt my career, and then I just didn't know how to erase it all."

"We can't. But we can move on." He lifted hopeful brows. "I'll prove myself however you want. I'll swear never to publish a word about any of this—the theory was ours, and I was an idiot to ever claim it was just mine. But it can be yours. Just yours."

"No." She rested a hand on his chest. "You still have a dissertation to write. You use it."

His shoulders eased down. "I don't really want a doctorate. Why bother? I've got a showboat, a museum...that's what I always wanted. You publish it, baby."

She bit her lip, looking up into his eyes. "How about... *we* publish it? Together?"

"Really?" After another few seconds of staring into Theresa's eyes, he looked at the Inn Crowd. "Will you let us make scans of your half of the script, ladies?"

"We'll let you have the original." Janice grinned.

They laughed again, looked at each other again. Theresa blushed. "Two halves, back together. Pretty fitting, I guess."

Thank You, Father God. Janice eased out a long breath. That had gone far better than she'd dared to hope.

A light tapping sounded on the door, and Leila poked her head in. She grinned when she saw her uncle and aunt standing there, still with their arms around each other. "Hey, not to interrupt, but the intermission's about over. You gonna come out and hear my big lines, Uncle Keith?"

"Oh my goodness. Leila." Theresa blinked rapidly and pressed a hand to her cheek. "Look at you, all grown up. I couldn't quite believe it was you last week. If I hadn't seen your mother, I don't think I would have made the connection. You were brilliant."

"And I need to see you in action." Keith moved forward, tugging Theresa along with him. "Come on, honey. I'm sure we can find you a chair."

Chuckling, Janice fell in behind Tess to follow them out, though she paused when she realized LuAnn wasn't right behind her. "You coming, Lu?"

"Hmm?" Her friend blinked, then smiled. "Yeah. I was just wondering. About Prudence and Jason. If this happened in 1851, it wasn't all that long before they got married. Do you ever wonder how they came to fall in love?"

"I have. But I bet you've come up with a better story than what I could." She linked their arms together as they moved to where Tess waited for them. "You can weave it for us after the play tonight."

LuAnn laughed and waved a guest into the café ahead of them. "I'll come up with something grand. Even so, it'll probably fall short of reality. Fiction usually does."

Chapter Eighteen

September 2, 1851

Prudence strode onto the porch of the farmhouse, well familiar with it after a summer of frequent visits. She hummed as she went, giving only a cursory knock upon the swinging door before opening it and letting herself inside.

Jason would likely not be in here anyway. He'd be out in the barn this time of day, determined to do his part despite the fact that he couldn't yet move around without the aid of a crutch or cane.

He may never walk unaided again, Mercy's husband had said. And even if he did, his leg would likely always trouble him if he overexerted himself. There would be no more midnight jaunts through the forest for him.

That pained him more than the injury itself, Prudence knew. He had whispered as much a month ago, while he still sat with the plaster cast holding him captive, unable to do any of the work he so loved. *Helpless,* he had all but spit more than once.

Prudence had stopped by nearly every day to lend a hand to his sister, who had brought her two small children and come to care for him while he was laid up. Neighbor men had made sure his crops were planted and the animals tended.

The Friends had banded together around him and never breathed a word about Prudence's supposedly rebellious trip to the theater. Oh, those two businessmen had paid Anna Barton a visit that very night, but Mercy had apparently interrupted their concerned diatribe by bursting in and relaying the news of Jason's injury and Prudence's role in getting him to help, and the men had either realized what she'd really been about or decided her aid of the Cause had been more important than any minor transgression.

The kitchen was sunny and clean but quiet. Too quiet. Sarah and her children had left yesterday, driving their creaking wagon the ten long miles back to their own farm. A shame—Prudence had greatly enjoyed getting to know Jason's sister.

She slid her basket onto the table and set about unloading the day's supplies. Bread, fresh from the oven and wrapped in a towel. A pat of butter, since his dish had looked low yesterday. A bowl of berries she and Anna had picked in yesterday's twilight.

A shuffling step from outside pulled her back to the door, the berries still in her hand. Jason was making his way to the house from the barn, his brows knotted. Was his leg bothering him more than usual today? She abandoned her basket and stepped back outside. "How does thee fare today, Jason Willard?"

His mouth puckered to match his brow upon spotting her. Odd. He hadn't growled over her visits since that first week—when he'd growled over everything, he was in so much pain. He gripped his cane hard, each step deliberate.

"What is thee doing here?" he demanded as he reached the porch steps.

She frowned in response. "The same thing I have been doing here every day for the last three months. Seeing that thee has a meal on the table for thy noon repast and tidying thy house."

He shook his head. "Thee cannot keep doing such a thing now, with Sarah gone. It isn't seemly."

Then why had Anna not said so? "How is it unseemly for one neighbor to look after another? I know well that Catherine Miller is bringing thy supper and that Nancy Baines will be—"

"That is different." He mounted the stairs—a halting movement, but one he'd mastered. Now that he was closer, she could see that his eyes twinkled beneath his frown.

Prudence's pulse kicked up. He'd grown no less handsome as she came to know him more. Her reactions to him no less intense. "I fail to see how."

He plucked a berry, so deep a purple it was nearly black, from the bowl and popped it into his mouth, smiling around it. "Because I have not asked to call at either of their houses."

"Thee has…what?" Her voice came out breathy. Embarrassingly so.

But still he smiled, looking down into her eyes with sunshine in his. Chased by a few clouds, but still. "I am not the man I was. But—"

"Nonsense! Thee is everything thee has always been. Or more. Thee has sacrificed for what thee believes in."

His smile deepened. "Will thee let me finish, Prudence Barton?"

She buttoned her lips and held the bowl of fruit against her middle.

He chuckled. "But I am a wise enough man to know when God has placed a blessing in my path. I spoke to thy guardian in town this morning. If thee is willing to suffer the attentions of a crippled farmer, I would consider it a pleasure to get to know thee more deeply."

"Thee would?" If she held the bowl any tighter, she'd likely break it and send blackberries rolling, but she couldn't convince her fingers to relax. "Truly? Will thee come tonight? To…to call?"

Still grinning, he wrenched the bowl of berries from her. Perhaps because he could foresee their plight, or perhaps because he wanted another. But no, he set it on the wide porch railing and took her hand in his. "Truly, yes. Tonight…no." He squeezed her fingers. "I will have visitors here tonight. In fact…I think thee and Anna will not be home either. She has already agreed to help these visitors find the farm. With thy help, that is. If thee will give it."

Her fingers wove through his. Exactly as she had dreamed so many times. And yet it felt nothing like she'd imagined. His hands weren't knotted like Anna's. Not small and smooth like Mercy's. They were large, strong, work-roughened, and oh so warm. Her fingers felt small and protected within his. Quavering and yet sure. Unfamiliar and yet...as if that were exactly where they belonged.

And he was sharing *that* with her. His work. The work she so wanted to belong to as well.

She tried to summon her most serious look, but she well knew a smile snuck in at the corners of her mouth. "These friends will have my help, to be sure. And thee, Jason Willard...can come and call tomorrow then."

In a move that melted her very bones, he raised her hand and pressed his lips to one of her knuckles. "Tomorrow cannot come soon enough."

"Wait a minute!" One of the audience members stood up after the whodunit had been announced, looking half irritated and half amused.

Janice shifted to where she could see who it was, smiling when she recognized Ruby from church. She thought she'd recognized the voice.

Ruby wagged a finger toward Keith and Theresa. "You mean to tell me it wasn't one of them? But I thought for sure— didn't you hear what they said?"

At her place in the front, Heidi put her hands on her hips and sent a mock glare at Keith.

He didn't miss a beat. "We, madam, were what is commonly referred to as the red herrings in the production. Just there to throw you off the scent."

Ruby scowled, then laughed and sat back down. "Here I was really looking forward to one of those cakes!"

Janice made a mental note. Ruby's birthday was coming up soon. She'd have to borrow Winnie's recipe and make her a cake.

The prizes were handed out, Heidi made the same closing statements she had last week, and Janice let out a happy sigh as the guests all stood, some heading immediately for the exit and others milling about, chatting.

Leila sidled her way over to her father and uncle's table, right in front of where Janice stood with Tess and LuAnn. She was beaming, and rightfully so. She'd done an amazing job again.

Ian stood to give her a hug. "So proud of you, baby girl! You were fantastic."

"You really were." Keith took his turn at a hug next and then propelled her toward Theresa. "Sure I can't lure you away for the summer?"

Leila laughed.

Her father punched his brother in the arm. "No way, no how, bro. She'll be in New York soon enough. This summer, she's ours."

Theresa pulled back from the quick hug, her eyes wide. "New York? Where are you going?"

"Well, I got into Juilliard and Barnard. Both are awesome, of course—"

"Juilliard?" Her aunt looked appropriately impressed. "Oh, sweetie, if you got in there, you have to go!"

Leila ducked her head. "We haven't dismissed it. But I got a better deal from Barnard..."

"What?" Keith was frowning. "How much of a better deal are we talking here? Because unless its tens of thousands a year, you can't let that stand between you and your dream school. You've been talking about wanting to go to Julliard since you were ten."

Leila shrugged, glanced quickly at her father, and pasted on a smile. "I have. And when we visited—it's awesome. But so is Barnard. I know I'll be perfectly happy there if it's where I end up going."

Keith looked far from convinced. He glared at his brother. "How much difference are we talking? Seriously."

Ian sighed. "Five thousand a year. I know it doesn't sound like a lot, but—"

"We'll pay it. Lend it, give it, whatever." Theresa elbowed Keith in the ribs. "Right? I know your showboat's doing okay, and I have that inheritance from my grandmother I'm not using."

"No." Ian held up a hand. "We can't—"

"Of course you can," Keith jumped in. "It's not like I have kids right now to be saving for. Take it, bro. Let our girl have her dream. We can worry about payback later." Keith said it easily, simply, as if it were the simplest thing in the world to promise twenty grand over the next four years.

Maybe it was, when it mattered this much. Because the moment her father nodded, Leila broke into a shout as joyous as the one Theresa had released when she realized her theory was right. She hugged her family all again and then, apparently in need of even more, launched herself at Janice.

Laughing, her arms closed around her young friend. "Good for you, sweetie," she whispered into her ear. "I'm so happy for you."

Leila pulled away with a bounce. "I have to go find Mama." And she was off, tearing through the café with waving arms and happy shouts for her mother.

Ian was sending his brother a dubious look, aimed half at Theresa. "Are you sure about this? I mean, you two . . ."

"We'll have plenty to work through." Theresa patted Keith's chest. "But Leila we can agree on. As I told you when first we met, Ian, that's some girl you've got there."

"Yeah." Ian's look became fond and warm. "Yeah, she is."

Janice drew in a happy breath and moved when her friends did to gather a few coffee cups and dessert plates to carry into the kitchen. Contentment swelled up in her chest. Not the kind that came just from having these friends to live life beside her. Not the kind that came from seeing happy swarms of people in their inn, the one they'd built together. Not even the kind on behalf of Heidi, at knowing her dream was coming true just as much as Leila's was.

The kind that came from knowing she'd done right. She'd corrected a wrong in her thinking, and it had resulted in new friends. Friends who really were extraordinary. Who were willing to work and sacrifice for their dreams.

She smiled at Tess and LuAnn as they pushed into the kitchen. Those were the best kinds of friends. "So, Lu, do you have our romantic tale ready for us?"

LuAnn grinned and brushed a silver lock away from her cheek. "I think I might. But I feel like it needs a footnote if I'm going to link it to this adventure they apparently had."

Tess slid her load of dishes to the counter by the sink. "What kind of footnote?"

"Well…" LuAnn leaned a hip against the counter and looked up, lips pursed. "I'm still not sure how half that script ended up in Canada, and the other half here, hidden in Mother Goose rhymes."

Janice shrugged. "If I were to guess, I'd say it had to be Virgil. He wrote the inscription to Oswald in the front, right? And then apparently came back here. So it stands to reason."

Tess stacked LuAnn's dishes with hers and reached for Janice's. "Probably. But ten years afterward, if we interpreted that entry correctly. That's a long time to wonder."

"Yeah." Janice smiled. "But I have to think the answer would be all the sweeter after the wait, when so many times they never got any answers at all. Don't you think?"

LuAnn nodded, smiling too. "Yeah. I think so."

May 20, 1861

Prudence led the way through the creaking swinging door of the house she'd called home for close to nine years now. Given the guest trailing her, she couldn't help but travel a decade into the past, when she'd been but a young woman trying to gain Jason Willard's attention. Tending him here alongside his sister during his convalescence. She'd scarcely seen the interior of this house for the year following, until she crossed its threshold as a bride.

Now she knew every plank, every crack, every cranny. She'd put her own touches on every surface.

She'd spent a decade loving the man who had suffered so much pain because of a slip of memory Virgil Sullivan had made. But she offered her guest a smile and a seat at the table. "Can I get thee a drink? Or something to eat? I have a strawberry pie made fresh yesterday."

Virgil smiled. "Well now, I don't suppose I could rightly turn that down."

Prudence turned to retrieve and slice the pie, her attention going out the window as she worked. Jason had spotted her coming up the lane, she knew. He'd paused out in the fields, raising a hand in greeting. He wouldn't know who the man accompanying her was, but he would hurry in to find out.

And indeed, there he came now. She scooped out a second serving of pie and prayed with every motion that Jason's shock wouldn't be too great. He had long ago forgiven the man's mistake, she knew. But they'd never heard from him, and had both wondered over the years whether he had been a true friend. Whether he'd led those brothers to safety or if they'd been caught. Whether they would ever see him again.

The last question was certainly answered.

Prudence slid the plates of pie onto the table just as Jason came inside, his smile freezing for a moment as he caught sight of the man sitting there. He seemed to search long and hard for a name to go along with the face before realization visibly dawned. He moved forward with a hand held out. "Virgil Sullivan."

"Mr. Willard." Virgil had taken to his feet and reached out to accept Jason's hand. "You can't know how good it is to see you, alive and healthy. So many times I wondered if you made it."

"We have wondered the same, in regards to thy mission. Please, sit. What brings thee back to Marietta? The theater?"

While the men sat, Prudence poured glasses of fresh milk for each and then slid into an empty chair.

Virgil was shaking his head. "No. Our boat's been requisitioned by the army for troop transports—I'm delivering it downriver for that purpose. But I couldn't resist a stop in Marietta. To visit. And to give you something."

He reached into the small bag he carried with him and pulled out a curious packet of papers. Some sort of pamphlet, perhaps? But it looked as though it was missing its cover.

He slid it onto the table with a sheepish smile. "It's the script. From the play we did that night. We tore it in two when we finally got them to Canada. Oz kept half, and I kept half. As a reminder of our journey along the Ohio."

"Oz?" Prudence drew her brows together.

"Oswald Green—the older of the brothers we helped that night."

Jason laughed. "We never learned their names. We have been praying for them these many years, but without names."

"Oz and Jemmy," Virgil provided.

"They made it then? To Canada?"

"Safe and sound. They spent the summer with us, posing as our servants on the showboat, then we delivered them across the border with nary a problem"—Virgil smiled—"but not before we instilled in young Oz a love of theater. He's working in the Toronto theater world now. Even trying his hand at writing plays, I believe. Oh." His face fell. "But you all probably don't really approve of that. We didn't realize at the time that Quakers disapprove of the theater. If we'd known…"

"It doesn't matter." Jason smiled and cut off a bite of pie. "We will not judge others for such things. Thee saved two lives with thy theater."

Virgil's face remained grave. "And nearly ended yours. I pray you've forgiven me, my friend. I never meant you harm."

"There's nothing to forgive. We were all doing what the Lord led. Mistakes were made, but..." Jason reached out and took Prudence's hand. "That one opened my eyes to how remarkable a woman my Prudence is. I ought to be thanking thee for it."

Prudence gave his fingers a squeeze, returned his smile, and then reached for the script. They shouldn't keep it here in the house, of course. It wouldn't do to have anything related to the stage around, given that there was an injunction against such things in their faith. She would find a safe place to store it, one of these days. And in the meantime, she thumbed through it, a few distant memories arising as she read the words upon the page and heard them instead in the voices of the actors. "The other players. Thy family?"

"All of them, yes. Parents, brothers and sisters, even my aunt. I was the youngest. And not trusted again with such important lines for years to come, I can assure you."

Prudence chuckled as she found the third act, where Fiddle came onto the scene. His lines weren't typed like the rest of it, just hastily scrawled in a script that was nearly illegible. But there it was, nonetheless. *South*, it said, where he'd said *north*.

He'd been a true friend. And would remain so.

Dear Reader,

For a brief time, between the ages of eleven and thirteen, I decided I was going to be an actress—in addition to a novelist, of course. I set upon my path with determination, auditioning for a few local productions. I'd say I landed the roles I wanted, but frankly, I think everyone who auditioned got a part. Still, I enjoyed my brief tenure upon the stage and the theater classes I took in high school, even though by then I'd decided that acting was *not* my calling.

Still, I have a love and appreciation for the dramatic arts, and as I sat down to brainstorm this book, I was thrilled with the idea of bringing the stage to the inn—literally! But as I focused on Janice and her role with this fledgling theater group, I also knew I wanted to talk about something I'm far too often guilty of—seeing the face instead of the heart. A theme especially appropriate in a story about people who can so easily shift the face they present. I hope you enjoyed Janice's blossoming understanding of the other characters.

As for the theory that traveling theaters—very popular groups in the nineteenth century—may have played a role in the Underground Railroad...well, there's no evidence that they did. But there's also nothing saying they didn't, so my writer's imagination had a lot of fun with that possibility!

Until next time,
Roseanna

ABOUT THE AUTHOR

Roseanna M. White is a best-selling, Christy Award–nominated author who has long claimed that words are the air she breathes. When not writing fiction, she's homeschooling her two kids, editing, designing book covers, and pretending her house will clean itself. Roseanna is the author of a slew of historical novels that span several continents and thousands of years. Spies and war and mayhem always seem to find their way into her books...to offset her real life, which is blessedly ordinary. You can learn more about her and her stories and sign up for her newsletter at roseannamwhite.com/.

THE PEOPLES BANK THEATRE

Theater has long been present in Marietta, Ohio. In 1911, the town built its first permanent theater, a destination for local productions, traveling companies, magic lantern projections, and silent movies. The original building burned down in 1917, but the C&M Amusement Company vowed to rebuild it bigger and better. And they did, opening the so-dubbed Hippodrome Theatre in 1919. One of the largest theaters in the Midwest at the time, this grand building was one of the few that could host even the largest Broadway plays, and the theater even had its own five-piece orchestra. For the next several decades, the Hippodrome, renamed the Colony Cinema in 1949 after a thorough remodel, reigned as one of the finest theater establishments to be found, even hosting movie premiers that brought screaming fans into Marietta's streets. The theater changed hands several times over the years, but when a broken boiler threatened to shut the place down for good in 1980, a determined local who had long worked there stepped in and bought the building—the first local owner. She could manage to run it only a few years, however, before astronomical heating costs forced her to close its doors. A local businessman then bought the building in the hopes that eventually it could be restored. After more than fifteen years, the theater association managed to raise enough funds to do just that, re-opening as the Peoples Bank Theater in 2016. This gorgeous building can now once again host movies, plays, recitals, concerts, graduations, magic acts, and touring performances, bringing the dramatic arts to vivid life again in Marietta. To find out more, visit peoplesbanktheatre.com

Something Delicious from our Wayfarers Inn Friends

Strawberry Scones

Ingredients:

2½ cups flour

½ cup sugar

½ teaspoon salt

½ teaspoon baking soda

1 teaspoon baking powder

8 tablespoons cold butter,
  cut into small pieces

⅔ cups cream + 1 table-
  spoon cream, separated

1 egg

8 medium-sized strawberries,
  minced

Strawberry Glaze:

2 strawberries, minced

2 cups powdered sugar

1 tablespoon cream

Instructions:

Preheat oven to 400 degrees. Line a baking sheet with parchment paper.

In a large bowl, combine flour, sugar, salt, baking soda, and baking powder. Cut in butter until the mixture resembles coarse crumbs, with some lumps the size of peas.

In a separate bowl, combine ⅔ cup cream and the egg. Add the strawberries. Pour into the dry mixture and mix until just combined. Transfer to a floured surface and lightly form into a disc. Cut the disc into 12 wedges or circles. Brush tops with the remaining 1 tablespoon cream. Bake for 12 minutes.

While the scones cool, make the glaze. In a small bowl, whisk together the strawberries, powdered sugar, and cream until you have a smooth glaze. Pour 1 tablespoon of glaze over the top of each scone. Let set and serve either warm or at room temperature.

Read on for a sneak peek of another exciting book
in the Secrets of Wayfarers Inn series!

STOLEN GOODBYES
by Beth Adams

The blast of cold air felt heavenly as LuAnn stepped inside the coffee shop. Outside, the day was hot and muggy, but inside Jeremiah's, it was cool and quiet, and the whole place smelled like rich espresso. LuAnn took a deep inhale and let it out slowly, then she moved toward a round table against the big plate-glass windows right by the door, where the summer sunshine poured in.

This was what she needed. A good, strong cup of coffee and a chat with a good friend. That would pull her out of the funk she had settled into this morning. It had been over a year since her mother's death, and yet LuAnn still missed her every day. Memories would come back to her at the oddest times—the way her mom would have laughed at something on television, or a song that reminded LuAnn of childhood—and her grief would come rolling back.

And it was no surprise that she was feeling particularly tender today. The estate had recently been settled, and LuAnn had finally worked up the courage to start cleaning out the storage unit where she'd stored the things from her mother's apartment in the dark days after the funeral. It needed to be done. She was glad for all the reminders of her mother's life, and she had packed the trunk of her car full of old letters and books. But she was still feeling a bit off-balance, haunted by the memories and waves of emotions that she wasn't quite sure how to process.

Now she pulled her wallet out of her purse, walked toward the counter, and scanned the board over the register. Coffee would help. What sounded good? Something cold, she decided.

"Hi there," the barista said. He had a stud in his chin, and part of a tattoo peeked out from under his sleeve. Some kind of dragon? LuAnn couldn't be sure, but she was pretty sure she had met him before. Micah, she thought his name was. He was a computer science major at a local college, if she was remembering correctly. "What can I get for you?"

"Could I get an iced latte?" Those frothy frozen blended concoctions looked good, but they were full of sugar, and she knew the smarter choice would be the simpler drink.

"Coming right up. I'll bring it to your table." Micah indicated the spot where she'd set her purse down.

"Thank you." LuAnn paid for her drink, then turned and looked around the small coffee shop. She loved the scraped hardwood floors, the exposed brick walls, and the mismatched tables and chairs that gave the place a homey feel. There were only a few other patrons at the moment—a guy typing away on his laptop, and a couple of women chatting about their children in the corner. LuAnn recognized one of them as Ruby Meyers, a friend of Janice's from church, though she didn't know the other woman.

LuAnn dropped her wallet into her purse and checked her watch. She was a few minutes early. She decided she had time to run to the restroom before Brad was due to arrive. She ducked down the hallway at the back that led to the kitchen and went into the bathroom. When she came out a few minutes later, she glanced around the large open room to see if Brad had arrived yet. She didn't see Brad, but—

Who was that? There was a man standing next to her table, and he was—

"Hey!" LuAnn called out. The man yanked his hand out of her purse and immediately started moving toward the door. "Hey! What are you doing?" The other patrons turned to her, but they didn't seem to see what was happening. "Stop!" She moved toward him, but before she could cross the room, he was out the door.

Micah, finally seeming to realize what was going on, raced out from behind the bar and crossed the floor in a few long strides. He yanked open the door and followed the man, who had turned left, headed away from the river. LuAnn followed just behind, but after a few steps, she was out of breath. Micah was much quicker, even in heavy combat boots. She watched as he ran down the block, chasing after the man, threading around the tourists that crowded the sidewalks, but the man was quickly gone from view.

LuAnn wasn't sure what else to do, so she turned around and went back inside the coffee shop. The women in the corner and the guy at his laptop were all staring at her, eyes wide.

"Did he take anything?" Ruby asked.

"I don't know." LuAnn stepped back to her table. "But I think so."

She had changed out her typical black leather purse for a structured canvas bag with blue canvas handles after Memorial Day. It felt summery and light—and, she now realized with a sinking heart—had no zipper, and was totally open to anyone who wanted to look or reach in. She saw that her phone was still tucked into an inside pocket, but when she shoved aside her sunglasses, keys, notebook, and various pens, she saw that her wallet was missing. "My wallet is gone."

"Oh no." Ruby's friend was on her feet and by LuAnn's side quickly.

LuAnn felt more and more foolish by the second. Why had she left her purse just sitting there? This was small-town Ohio, and it always felt so safe that she just hadn't thought...But of course there was crime here, just like everywhere else. The mysteries she and her friends had encountered in the past year had proven that. And she'd left the bag unattended right in the front window, where anyone walking by could have seen it. It would only take a second to duck into the coffee shop and grab the wallet. It could happen so fast no one would even notice. Apparently, no one else had. She dug through her purse again, but that seemed to be the only thing that was missing.

"I'm so sorry," Ruby's friend said. "I looked up when he came in, but I didn't really pay attention. I wish I'd watched a bit more carefully."

"It's not your fault," LuAnn said. "I shouldn't have left it sitting there."

"Hopefully Micah will have caught him," Ruby said. The man at the laptop had put in earbuds and was back to typing away.

"Let's hope." Still, LuAnn pulled out her phone and unlocked it in case she needed to call the police. A moment later, Micah appeared in the shop window, shaking his head. LuAnn's heart sank.

"I'm sorry," he said as he stepped in. "I thought I was going to catch him, but then he disappeared into the crowd. He must have turned off somewhere. I don't know where he went."

"Thank you for trying," LuAnn said.

"I'm really sorry it happened. This place is usually so safe—"

"I should have known better," LuAnn said with a sigh. She'd traveled all over the world, from Thailand to Rome to Scandinavia to Costa Rica, and she'd never had her wallet stolen. And here she'd basically left the door wide open for the thief.

"You should cancel your credit cards right away," Ruby said.

"Best to call the police first," her friend said.

LuAnn nodded. "I'll start there." She moved toward the door so her phone call wouldn't disturb everyone else, but just as she was about to step outside, Brad appeared in the window.

"What's going on?" he said, entering the shop. The smile that had been on his face a moment before dropped as he looked around.

"I made a silly mistake and left my purse unattended," LuAnn said and explained what had happened. Brad used his phone to call the Marietta police while LuAnn used her phone to find the phone numbers for her bank and credit card companies. It only took a few minutes to cancel the cards, and she was just hanging up when Chief Mayfield strode into the coffee shop, followed by Officer Randy Lewis.

Chief Mayfield looked at LuAnn. "What's this I hear about a wallet going missing?"

LuAnn tried to laugh, but she knew it sounded hollow. She explained what had happened.

Randy got his notebook out. "Can you describe the man?"

"He was pretty tall," LuAnn said.

"With wide shoulders," Ruby added.

"And long legs," Micah called from behind the bar. "He runs really quickly."

"What was he wearing?" Chief Mayfield asked. The police chief was probably in his mid-fifties, with gray threaded through his dark brown hair. His paunch strained the fabric of his gray police uniform.

"He was wearing a blue shirt," LuAnn said. "And khaki pants."

"What color blue? Light? Dark?"

"Dark," LuAnn said at the same time that Ruby answered, "Light."

"I thought it was more of a grayish color," Micah said. "But he was wearing a hat."

"Yes, he definitely had a hat on," LuAnn said. "A light-colored one. Straw, I think."

"A straw hat?" Randy looked at her skeptically.

"Not like one of those old ones you'd put on a scarecrow. Like a fedora."

"A straw fedora?" The officer didn't look any more convinced.

"That's right," Ruby's friend agreed. "That's exactly what it was."

"They're really trendy," Micah added from behind the counter.

"My brother, Grant, has one," Brad said.

Randy looked around the room, from LuAnn to Brad to Micah to Ruby. Then he shrugged and wrote "straw fedora" on his notepad. "How old was he?" he asked.

"It's hard to say," LuAnn said. "I really only saw him from the back."

"I saw him. I would guess fifties," Ruby said.

"No way," Micah called. "He has to be younger, based on how fast he got away." Micah explained how he had chased the guy and described where he saw him last.

Randy kept writing. "Can you describe the wallet?"

LuAnn told him it was made from black leather, and she gave him the brand and described the silver clasp.

"Anything valuable inside?"

"About forty dollars in cash." She shrugged. "The rest was all replaceable."

Chief Mayfield turned to Micah. "Do you have security cameras in here?"

Micah shook his head. "We don't. But I think the hardware store might." He gestured to the store across the street.

"We'll check with them," Chief Mayfield said. "Is there anything else you can think of? Any way to identify him?"

LuAnn thought for a minute and then shook her head.

"Anyone else?" Everyone, even the guy with the headphones on, shook their heads.

"We'll do the best we can," Chief Mayfield said. "But it's not a lot to go on."

"Best thing to do is cancel the credit cards and report them stolen," Randy said. "That way if someone tries to use one, the credit card company will let you know."

"Already taken care of," LuAnn said.

"Well, in that case, we'll see what we can turn up."

"Thank you," LuAnn said. She knew they didn't have a lot of clues, and she suspected chances were slim that she would see the wallet again, but she tried to remain hopeful. The police promised to be in touch, and then they headed out.

"I'm sorry that happened," Brad said, sinking down into the chair across from LuAnn.

LuAnn shrugged. "Like I said, I should have known better. And hopefully they'll get it back."

Micah appeared with a cup and set it in front of LuAnn. "Here's that iced latte." He gave her a sad smile. It was a good thing she'd already paid for it. "And what can I get you, sir? It's on the house, for the trouble."

Brad ordered a plain iced coffee but insisted on paying, and a moment later he and LuAnn were sitting at the table ready to chat about the reason they had met there in the first place.

"There are just a few details we wanted to run past you before Saturday." LuAnn pulled her notebook out of her bag and set it on the table. "We're working hard to pull it all together, but with such a short time frame we need to make sure we nail everything down quickly."

"Great. I'm anxious to see what you've come up with. Whatever it is, I know Lauren will be pleased."

LuAnn had heard Brad talk about his goddaughter Lauren a few times. She was the daughter of his best friend from childhood, Mark Haywood, who lived outside Cleveland. LuAnn knew Brad took his role as godfather seriously, especially since Lauren's mother had passed away from an aggressive form of breast cancer a few years back. He kept in contact with his goddaughter and saw her as much as he could, and he'd recently shown off photos of her nursing school graduation. When he'd come to the inn a few weeks back and asked for their help, they hadn't hesitated. Lauren was newly engaged, he'd said, and she wanted to have the wedding quickly, before her fiancé left for basic training. Lauren had scrambled to find a venue that was open at such short notice, and Brad had suggested Wayfarers Inn, the bed and breakfast LuAnn ran with her friends Janice and Tess. They'd agreed to host the reception and had worked hard to pull it together quickly. Since Lauren and her family were two and a half hours away, and because Lauren didn't seem to have strong feelings about the details, Brad was dealing with much of the wedding minutiae.

LuAnn made another note. "Do you have a final count for the guests yet?"

"Not final, but Lauren says it's looking like it will be somewhere around fifty."

"All right." LuAnn looked up. "If she gives you an update, just let us know, but for now, we'll work with that." She flipped to a page of her notebook where she'd sketched out the inn and its grounds. "With that number, I think it would be best to have the tables set up here, under the trees"—she pointed to where she'd sketched out long tables on the lawn under the live oaks—"as long as the weather is nice. It would be a bit cramped inside, but if it rains, we'll make it work."

"I think that sounds beautiful," Brad said. "Lauren will love it."

"We'll keep the linens simple—just white—and we'll use fresh flowers along the tables." They'd work with Tie The Knot, the local wedding shop that rented linens and tables and other party necessities, to get everything set up.

LuAnn took a long pull on the straw in her cup. The coffee was cool and sweet and exactly what she needed. "Do you want to run it past her to make sure?"

"You ladies will make it look beautiful. I trust you."

"Do you think she'd prefer a more formal look? With more structured flowers and real vases? Or do you think she'd want something a little more laid-back? Maybe daisies and black-eyed Susans in mason jars?"

"Lauren isn't fussy, so whatever you think is best."

LuAnn clicked her pen. He'd said that a few times, and though she trusted him, she still had a difficult time believing that Lauren wouldn't be just a bit fussy about the details for her wedding. But Brad had insisted Lauren was busy starting a new job and buying a home and planning for her soon-to-be husband to be gone for months on end, and she didn't have time to worry about decisions like this. She would simply have run off to the courthouse to do the deed if her father hadn't insisted on a real wedding. Lauren had acquiesced, but Brad said Lauren had assured him more than once that she didn't care what kind of tablecloths and flowers were used so long as she ended up married to Ethan at the end of the day. It was a nice sentiment, and LuAnn wanted to believe it was true, but she had yet to meet a bride who truly meant it.

"All right." LuAnn turned the page of her notebook. "Now, the menu. You said you were thinking of starting with an appetizer course, followed by a full dinner."

"If that works for you." Brad shrugged. "If it were up to Lauren, it would be hot dogs and watermelon, but both her father and I think a proper sit-down meal will be best."

LuAnn nodded, uncertain. She thought a proper wedding dinner was best too, but she wanted to make sure Lauren was happy with the reception. If she wanted something less fussy, shouldn't they listen?

"We can do hot dogs," LuAnn said. "We could even do gourmet hot dogs, with lots of exotic toppings, to make it fun."

Brad sighed and shook his head. "I have no doubt you could," he said slowly. "But..." He picked up his drink and took a long sip. LuAnn waited for him to go on, but he took his time.

"Both Mark and I think this is what her mother would have wanted," he finally said. "When Kelly was sick, I promised her I would take care of Lauren, and Kelly would never have let Lauren get away with hot dogs for her wedding dinner."

Ah. That was it. Brad was planning the wedding because Lauren's mother wasn't here to do it herself, and he wanted to do it the way Kelly would have wanted it done. It was touching, really. As long as Lauren was okay with the results.

"Okay then. I put together a couple of preliminary menus." She pulled out some pages she'd printed out. "This one is a little more Mediterranean, with feta puffs and shrimp and hummus as appetizers and fish for the main course. And this one is more all-American." She handed him the second menu, which featured sirloin tips and scalloped potatoes and biscuits.

"Let's go for All-American," Brad said. "Ethan is joining the army after all, and I know he likes hearty food."

LuAnn wrote it down. She was fond of steak and potatoes herself. But still, she hesitated. "Speaking of Ethan...Does he have an opinion about any of this?"

Something flitted across Brad's face. Some look she couldn't read. He lifted his cup and shook it, resettling the ice, and then took a sip. "I'm not really sure."

"Should we ask?" The mother of the bride may not be around to have opinions about this wedding, but would Ethan or his family have thoughts?

"I think it's fine without his input," Brad said. "Mark is the one paying for the wedding, after all. We don't need to get Ethan involved."

There it was again. Some emotion she couldn't name passed across his face as he said the name of the groom.

"What do you think of Ethan?" she asked carefully.

"Ethan?" Brad traced his initials in the condensation on the side of his cup. "He's fine."

There it was. Ethan, in Brad's eyes, was not fine.

"What is it?" LuAnn asked gently. "Why don't you like him?"

"I didn't say I didn't like him. He's a nice guy."

"But...?" LuAnn met Brad's eyes and didn't look away until, several seconds later, he looked down.

"But I don't know how Lauren is going to like military life," he finally said.

"It can be a hard life," LuAnn said. "But I suppose she knows what she's getting into."

"No one really knows what they're getting into when they get married," Brad said. "It's..."

LuAnn waited, hoping he would say more. She hadn't heard him say much about his wife, Stephanie, who had passed away four years ago, and hoped he would offer some insight now. But instead, he said, "Ethan is fine. It's just that, Lauren is so smart and so special. I thought she might find someone a little more..." He let his voice trail off, then said briskly, "Did you know she graduated at the top of her class? In high school and college too? And then she went on to nursing school, and of course she did fantastic there too."

"That's wonderful," LuAnn said. She thought she was beginning to see what was bothering him. "Will she be able to use her degree after they get married?"

"I don't see how, since they'll be moving every few years."

"Nurses are needed everywhere," LuAnn said gently.

Brad continued running his finger along the condensation on the outside of his cup and didn't answer. LuAnn understood a lot from what he didn't say.

"She must see something in him, if she's marrying him," she said.

"He's a good-looking guy." Brad shrugged. "But will that be enough a few years down the line, when he's off fighting some battle, and she's home alone with the kids for months on end?"

LuAnn wasn't sure how to answer. Truthfully, it sounded like a difficult life. But being a soldier was a noble profession, a sacrifice only the bravest, most selfless men and women were willing to make. But no one said Ethan would be in the military forever.

But that wasn't what was really at the root of Brad's unease.

"She could have had anyone, you know?" Brad said.

LuAnn nodded because she wasn't sure what else to do. "Well, she's chosen him. So let's make sure their wedding is as wonderful as we can make it, okay?" She said it with more enthusiasm than she truly felt.

"Yes," Brad said. "For Lauren, let's make it the most beautiful wedding this town has ever seen."

Find more inspiring fiction in these best-loved Guideposts series!

Tearoom Mysteries Series

Mix one stately Victorian home, a charming lakeside town in Maine, and two adventurous cousins with a passion for tea and hospitality. Add a large scoop of intriguing mystery and sprinkle generously with faith, family, and friends, and you have the recipe for *Tearoom Mysteries*.

Sugarcreek Amish Mysteries

Be intrigued by the suspense and joyful "aha" moments in these delightful stories. Each book in the series brings together two women of vastly different backgrounds and traditions, who realize there's much more to the "simple life" than meets the eye.

Mysteries of Martha's Vineyard

What does Priscilla Latham Grant, a Kansas farm girl know about hidden treasure and rising tides, maritime history and local isle lore? Not much—but to save her lighthouse and family reputation, she better learn quickly!

Mysteries of Silver Peak

Escape to the historic mining town of Silver Peak, Colorado, and discover how one woman's love of antiques helps her solve mysteries buried deep in the town's checkered past.

To learn more about these books, visit Guideposts.org/Shop